I0731467

BAD BISHOP

A PERFECT PLAY NOVEL

LAYLA REYNE

Bad Bishop

Copyright © 2022 by Layla Reyne

All rights reserved. No part of this book may be reproduced or transmitted in any form or by any means, electronic or mechanical, including photocopying, recording, or by any information storage and retrieval system without the written permission of the copyright owner, and where permitted by law. Reviewers may quote brief passages in a review.

Cover Design: Cate Ashwood Designs

Cover Photography: Wander Aguiar Photography

Editing: Susie Selva

Proofreading: Lori Parks

First Edition

October, 2022

E-Book ISBN: 978-1-7373524-7-1

Paperback ISBN: 978-1-7373524-8-8

This is a work of fiction. Names, characters, places, and incidents are either the product of the author's imagination or are used fictitiously. Any resemblance to actual persons living or dead, business establishments, events, or locales is entirely coincidental. All person(s) depicted on the cover are model(s) used for illustrative purposes only.

Content Warnings: explicit sex; explicit language; violence; trafficking; off-page death of a former spouse; instances and/or discussion of homophobia; and instances and/or discussion of depression and PTSD.

For my husband,
who kept me in the game with this one

ABOUT THIS BOOK

When a marriage of convenience becomes more than either husband bargained for...

Special Agent Levi Bishop needs to:
Keep his son and family safe.
Prove his boss was framed for a crime she didn't commit.
Convince his selfless cowboy husband that his needs matter too.
Make a bold play before love slips through his fingers.

Special Agent Emmitt Marshall needs to:
Protect his husband and stepson.
End the nightmare that's haunted him since his mentor's murder.
Hack through layers of deception to identify the real threat.
Stop hoping someone will choose him.

Marsh is determined to go it alone, to guard his family and his heart.

But Levi's life and heart are on the line too.
Cornered, Levi will chance any play to save the marriage
and man he needs.
Rings were exchanged and promises made.
Marsh kept up his end of the bargain.
Now it's Levi's turn.

Bad Bishop is the second book of the Perfect Play trilogy, a swoony, edge-of-your-seat M/M romantic suspense series featuring a marriage of convenience between two FBI agents determined to stop a common enemy—and to do right by each other.

ONE

LEVI WAS WORRIED—AND his list of troubles was long.

There was his too-quiet son staring out the back-seat window of the rented SUV. David had been talkative the first hour or so of the flight to Texas, humoring Lily and chatting tattoos and chess with Holt and Brax, but when Marsh had refused to give David his phone, all the fear and anger from earlier that morning, from their standoff in the airport, simmered again in his son's green eyes and stewed there the remainder of the flight and as they drove across the west Texas desert.

Their locked-down phones were another worry. The FBI agent in Levi understood why it was necessary—they didn't want to be tracked; burners were safer—but the son and brother in him worried his parents or sisters would forget to use the burners if an emergency arose. What if Orchard Investments or Eder Capital sent henchmen to breach Aunt Liz's compound? What if Aunt Liz and his mother tore each other, and the place, apart themselves?

What if Taco or Burrito slipped through the gates and got lost in Rancho Santa Fe?

And then there was the cowboy-sized worry in the driver's seat beside him. For someone who'd been so easy to read the past three weeks, even under his cocky cowboy persona, now Marsh, like their phones, was locked down tight, his moment of vulnerability on the plane a thirty-thousand-foot memory. It was impossible to tell what was going on behind his dark brown eyes, what thoughts were causing him to clench his jaw every few minutes, what wrong words Levi had said to cause Marsh to rebuild his walls. Did he even still want to fight for his case or for Levi and David?

Then of course there was the mountain of professional worry. Levi's boss was behind bars, framed for her boss's murder, his partner and another colleague were in the hospital, his home was a crime scene, they were missing prime suspects, and the bad guys had no doubt painted targets on his and Marsh's backs.

All that said, there was a more pressing worry at the top of Levi's list. That at any moment they'd hit a bump, take a turn too fast, and he'd paint the SUV's floorboards with what little food was left in his stomach. Fucking altitude sickness. It hadn't occurred to him that he'd have to deal with it in the Texas desert. A desert that was four thousand feet above the one he was used too. He was feeling every extra foot of elevation, his head dizzy, his breaths short, and his stomach woozy.

David's first words in hours were a welcome distraction. "What's that?" Arm stretched between the front seats, he pointed at the rocky outcrop ahead.

"Cathedral Mountain," Marsh replied, voice scratchy from disuse. "Home's not far now."

Levi wanted to ask more about the mountain and their surroundings, but Marsh slowed, turned on his blinker to signal Holt and Brax behind them, and turned off the highway onto a side road. If Levi had thought he was nauseous before, the bump and rumble across dry, packed earth was another level of hell. He laid a hand over his stomach, closed his eyes, and breathed deep.

"Almost there," Marsh assured him, and after mere minutes that felt like hours, the road beneath them finally leveled out again.

Levi eked open his eyes to a desert suddenly tinged with familiar deep pink. Bougainvillea wound through the gaps of the roadside fence, blooms bright in the afternoon sun. But Marsh's favorite flower was just the start of nature showing off. On the other side of the fence, the desert gave way to pops of orange, yellow, and purple among the tall grass and green brush, and in the approaching distance, thicker groves of mesquite and acacia trees swayed with the breeze.

"Why's it so much greener inside the fence?" David asked.

"Live water snakes through the property," Marsh said. "And we've put in decades of rehab and conservation work. Whatever we took out of the ground, we put back into it."

They crested a hill, and the knotted wood fence rose with them, rose higher still, curving and climbing vertical until it arched over a gravel drive, the hand-carved ranch gate dripping with magenta flowers. Beneath it, a metal gate retracted, and a palomino trotted through, its blond mane shining in the sun, the long blond hair of its rider likewise shimmering gold. Marsh turned into the drive and rolled down his window while David followed the earlier path of his arm, leaning forward between the seats to peer up at the words carved overhead. "Mi Herencia" he read aloud, then translated. "My heritage."

Levi chuckled, cautiously in case more than his laughter tried to escape. "You weren't kidding about Camilla giving your dad the middle finger."

The horse stuck its muzzle inside the open window, eager for Marsh's attention, while its rider's mischievous voice chimed from outside. "Giving that man the middle finger is my wife's favorite pastime."

"Isn't your dad dead?" David asked.

The rider leaned over the palomino's neck and peered inside Marsh's window. Light green eyes full of mirth danced beneath the brim of a straw hat. "One less asshole in the world."

David's eyes grew wide, and his ginger brows raced north. "Ohmigod."

Marsh sighed as he petted the horse's damp nose. "Mama, maybe wait until after introductions."

"No use hiding the ball, mijo." Irina then, and exactly as Marsh had described her. Frank and to the point, and trouble with a capital *T*. She cast her green gaze toward the SUV behind them. "Please tell me that sexy piece of Brooklyn ass is in the car behind you." An incorrigible flirt too apparently. Like mother like son.

"Brax is gay and very happily married."

"Does not negate the sexy or the fine ass."

Levi couldn't bite back his laugh, David either. Even Marsh's jaw loosened a fraction. Worth risking vomitus maximus. Marsh patted his stepmom's knee, same as he'd done the horse's nose. He spoke in a language Levi didn't recognize—Polish, he guessed—and whatever Marsh had said must have been good. Irina's smile brightened and she clasped his hand, squeezing tight. When Marsh spoke again, it was in English. "We should get to the house before Mom sends out a search party."

"Too right." Irina doffed her hat in Levi and David's direction, shot Brax a flirty wave, then trotted back through the gate. She waited long enough for their SUVs to drive through, for the lower gate to close behind them, then with a shout in that same foreign language from before, she double tapped the horse's sides and left them in the dust, riding full out.

David muttered a curse, and Levi was too busy gawking to correct him.

"That's another reason Mom fell in love with her," Marsh said. "Best rider either of us has ever seen."

They followed Irina's cloud of dust down the long entry road—past rolling hills and level grazing pastures, past cattle napping in the shade of massive solar panels, past water towers and silos, past countless rows of vegetables, corn, and grains—until a sprawling log cabin appeared ahead. Marsh swung their SUV around the circular drive and parked in front of the homestead's porch.

"You grew up here?" David asked, face practically pressed against the window.

"I did, but we've expanded over the years. When Mom bought it, the only structures were a V-shaped log cabin and a barn. We added two wings to the house so it's more of an X now, plus all the silos, outbuildings, and solar fields."

Levi was still taking it all in—the large A-frame at the center of the structure, the long, single-story wings to either side, the metal roof and stone foundation—when the front door swung open. A woman stepped out from under the porch's shade, and her resemblance to Marsh was uncanny. Tall and sturdy with big brown eyes, golden-brown skin, and thick black hair shot through with silver, the waves held back from her face by a pair of sunglasses on her head. Her most striking, most familiar feature was the one Levi hadn't seen on Marsh's face all day, a smile so full of joy and warmth that no one could look away. "You look just like her."

Grinning, Camilla descended the front porch steps and used every extra inch she had over Irina to crowd her wife back against the hitching post she'd tied her horse to and kiss her without a care in the world for their audience.

Eyes rolling closed, Marsh leaned his head back against the headrest. "In case the genetics didn't give it away." He flicked a hand their direction. "No use hiding the ball."

Sputtering, David turned beet red, hilariously caught between awestruck and mortified, awkward teen in full effect. The entirety of the scene caused Levi to laugh out loud, and his insides thankfully remained inside. Welcome relief from the day's tension rolled in with the uninhibited laughter, and beside him Marsh exhaled too, a long deep breath that relaxed his shoulders and jaw with it. He righted his head and smiled. "Welcome to Texas."

They piled out of the car, and while Levi felt emotionally more stable, he wasn't physically out of the woods yet. He wobbled on his feet, altitude still a factor, and steadied himself on the sideview mirror and David's open door. His hand nearly collided with David's, his son blinded by the midday sun, their sunglasses somewhere in the kitchen back home, left behind in the mad dash out of town. Marsh, however, seemed unaffected by the altitude and the blinding ball of light in the sky, not the least bit fazed by his missing white Stetson. He rounded the hood of the car and walked straight into Camilla's open arms.

"It's good to see you, mijo."

Marsh returned his mother's embrace, more of the day's tension seeping from his frame. "Thanks for accommodating us on such short notice."

She reared back and popped his shoulder. "Don't talk to me like I'm some goddamn distant relative. You don't need to give us notice to come home."

He lifted a brow, gaze sliding to where Irina remained lounged against the hitching post like she was waiting for her wife to come ravage her some more.

"Okay, an hour," Camilla conceded. "Just to be sure we're decent."

"Consider the thanks on our behalf," Brax said, joining their group with Lily on his hip, the toddler biting her lips and bouncing in his arms.

Camilla slapped his shoulder too. "You don't need to give notice either."

Lily finally exploded, stretching toward Camilla. "Mama Milla!"

Camilla caught her midlunge, swinging her high then into her arms, blowing a raspberry on her cheek. "Especially you!"

Drawn to the joy and warmth, Levi pried his fingers from the car and cautiously stepped forward. No wobbles. He grabbed David by the shoulder, just in case, and together they made it the few feet to Marsh's side. "I feel out gunned here," he said to Marsh. "I didn't bring flowers, and I don't have a cute ginger munchkin to offer."

"Hey!" David squawked.

Marsh reached around Levi to ruffle David's hair, and David's anger that had started to wane in the car ebbed some more. Taking advantage of the position and the lighter mood, Levi chanced leaning into Marsh's side. The move paid off, Marsh settling his arm across Levi's shoulders, the big body beside his loose for the first time since early morning.

Until his mother's "Mijo?" in that *oh shit Mom's onto me* tone clued them in that yes, Camilla was onto them. Her narrowed gaze was locked on Marsh's hand draped over Levi's shoulder. "Is that one of the rings Rio made? The ones we gave you for—"

"The smokin' hot blond is wearing the other one," Irina said as she pushed off the post.

David snickered. "Here we go."

Levi gave him a pop similar to the one Camilla had given Brax and Marsh.

Chuckling, Marsh tugged him closer, and Levi happily snuggled against his side. "The smokin' hot blond is married too." Levi tangled his fingers with Marsh's dangling ones, and Camilla's eyes went wide as did Marsh's smile. "Mom, Mama, I'd like to introduce you to Levi Bishop, my husband."

Camilla lowered her gaze, and Levi suddenly remembered the mountain of worry he'd blissfully forgotten for five minutes. Worried it had just gotten taller. Was Camilla disappointed—in Marsh, in him and David, in not being invited to the wedding? But then she crossed herself and started mumbling in rapid-fire Spanish Levi did under-stand. She wasn't disappointed at all.

"Did she just thank all the saints and declare this a holy day?" David asked, catching on too.

"She did," Irina said. "We didn't think our boy would ever settle down."

"Mama, it's not—"

Levi squeezed his hand, drawing Marsh's gaze, hoping the message in his was clear. None of that talk, not until after they had a talk first. One in which Levi needed to convince Marsh his feelings about them hadn't changed. If anything, they'd grown stronger. Levi was more certain than ever who he wanted as a partner in all aspects of his life. He just needed Marsh to be certain too.

Levi drew Marsh's hand to his lips, kissed his knuckles, then lowered their arms so he could step forward, hand outstretched to Camilla. "Levi Bishop." Then to Irina. "It's a pleasure to meet you both." Each handshake led to a hug, Camilla's sideways with Lily still on her hip, Irina's crushing. Levi swam in the warmth that crashed into his chest, that intensified when Marsh, with a soft smile that spoke of pride and affection, encouraged David forward. Levi waved him the rest of the way to his side. "And this is my son, David."

"He gots red hair too!" Lily exclaimed.

"I see that." Camilla's smile stretched wide. "Now I have two redheaded grandbabies!" She put her forehead to the side of Lily's, casting a mischievous glance David's way. "I wonder if the new one likes tamales as much as you do."

The teenage bottomless pit nodded eagerly, suddenly finding his appetite. "I'm from California. I will never say no to tamales."

"You'll fit right in," Irina said with a wink. "Let's go. You can help us roll them." She turned toward the house, following Camilla and Lily, and David turned his longing gaze on Levi, seeking permission to follow his stomach. Levi gave him the go-ahead, glad one of them could eat, the thought of food, even tamales, still making his stomach turn.

But while his stomach was in a bad place, his heart and soul were on a path to a better one. "Just like that?" Marsh's family had taken them in with open arms, no judgment, no questions asked. He was grateful to have that with his own family, but to have another chance at it… Could he be that lucky?

"Yep, just like that," Brax said as Holt carried a second load of computer and toddler gear past them. "You gave them what they've always wanted. Their son's happiness." He followed his husband inside, leaving Marsh and Levi alone for the first time in hours.

"I'm sorry," Marsh said, stepping closer. "I didn't have a chance to talk long before… to explain to them—"

"Let them be happy." Levi laid a hand over his chest, pleased when Marsh covered it with his. "Let all of us be happy. After the day we've had—hell, the past three weeks —we've earned it."

TWO

IF LEVI HAD THOUGHT the bougainvillea was extensive on the way into Mi Herencia, it was nothing compared to the wily plant's presence behind the sprawling ranch. From his spot at one end of the backyard picnic table, Levi spied magenta flowers scaling either corner of the house, framing the back door, and drowning a chicken coop in a nearby yard. No wonder their wedding venue in San Diego had caused Marsh to stumble. No wonder the pops of pink in Levi's backyard had also reminded him of home.

Levi was starting to understand the rest of it too, why Marsh had settled so easily in San Diego and into his and David's home. The desert landscape, the heat, the lived-in feel of the house. But there was something more about this place. Something magical in the tidy yet sprawling log cabin with its rustic charm, the abstract murals that decorated the walls and told the story of Marsh's family in hues of every color, the high-tech security and monitoring that were all Marsh, and the two women who had effortlessly wrapped Levi and David in their arms.

But along with the sense of magic came profound confusion, which had only continued to build as they'd settled in. Well, he and David had. Marsh, on the other hand, had ushered them into the charming house, guided them to safety, then had promptly run the opposite direction, out the back door, and onto a giant chestnut stallion, riding out to God only knew where on the property with Camilla. There'd been no time for conversations or explanations, not a minute to get their stories straight, not even a second for a kiss or a breather in each other's arms. Moments that Marsh was usually so keen to snatch like in the FBI bathroom after Levi had nearly been run over, or in the hotel room when Levi's world had been a circus, or any number of mornings on the patio over breakfast, or in the kitchen that night after June's wedding. Marsh was usually the one who made Levi slow down, so why was Marsh the one running now?

How did someone as loved as Marsh not think himself worthy of it?

That was the only explanation Levi could muster. That Marsh was sacrificing his own heart and happiness to protect Levi and David because he couldn't fathom Levi staying by his side after this morning. In truth, Levi was more afraid than ever to leave Marsh's side, to face their enemies alone or go back to the loneliness that had colored his world the past two years. Either of those prospects was enough to turn his already suspect stomach. He lifted a forkful of Texas caviar—maybe it would help; he usually loved the stuff—but one whiff and his stomach somersaulted. He hadn't felt this nauseous since that work conference he'd been to in Albuquerque years back.

"I can tell you've been learning from Marsh," Brax said at the other end of the table.

"Romantic chess," David replied.

Levi tuned into the exchange, desperate for a distraction. "Romantic chess?" He couldn't recall hearing that term before from any of the chess players in his life.

"Attacks and sacrifices," David said as he unwrapped tamale number three, clearly not afflicted with the same altitude sickness as Levi.

"Lots of bold sweeping moves," Holt added. On his lap, Lily made a bold move of her own, stretching for a crayon and nearly knocking over her father's soda. Holt shot out an arm faster than Levi would have imagined of a man so large and saved his drink. "Often quick," he said with a laugh.

Was he talking about his save or the game? Because when it came to chess, it seemed so slow to Levi, like Marsh and David were just staring at the board, moving at a snail's pace that was only slightly more exciting than golf. But the new term rattled something loose from his and Marsh's first meeting. "A theoretical novelty?" Levi said. "Is that romantic chess?"

Brax nodded. "One of the opening plays."

"But the move I just made was a desperado sacrifice," David said as he pumped his fist in the air. "I've never been able to pull it off against Marsh."

Levi shivered. He didn't want to think of the word sacrifice anywhere near Marsh or David. He didn't even want chessboards near them, but that seemed like an impossibility. He was impressed David could even look at one after Marsh's had almost exploded in his hands this morning. The memory of the near miss made Levi's stomach lurch.

Again. He let the conversation and his food go, surrendering his fork and napkin, sticking to careful sips of water instead.

Irina slid onto the bench opposite him. "Not a fan of tamales?"

"I am usually. But this altitude is tearing my stomach up."

"That's what I figured." She reached into her pocket and slid a familiar yellow tablet across the table. "Zofran. Will help with the—"

"Nausea," Levi said around the ache in his chest.

"You've dealt with altitude sickness before?"

"A work conference in Albuquerque. I forget how low we are in San Diego and how high other deserts can be." He picked up the pill. "But that's not why I know these." He curled his hand around the single tablet he'd counted out multiples of daily. "My late wife had cancer. She swore by these. Made chemo bearable for her."

Irina covered his other hand. "I'm sorry for your loss. Truly." Calm words, a gentle touch, Levi could see why she was good with animals. People too.

"Thank you." He swallowed the pill dry, then took a sip of water.

"Is it gonna make you more nauseous if I ask how my son proposed?"

And almost spit it out, laughter bubbling up. "Why would that make me nauseous?"

"Romantic chess and all that." She flapped a dismissive hand at the other end of the table, then leveled him with a far more interested stare. "And that boy tells his mother everything, which means there's more to this marriage than it seems since I haven't heard about you or your son until today."

Levi deflected, still needing to talk with Marsh before divulging details to Irina. "Marsh told me he and Camilla were tight." His gaze wandered the direction they'd ridden off. "But seeing them in action, how they moved around each other without words..." Visitors settled, black Stetson unpacked, canteens filled, horses saddled, and out they'd gone.

"It's always been that way with them. Short or long absences, it doesn't matter. He comes home and out they go. It's their time, together and with the land."

"I thought he was run—" He cut short the truth that had tried to slip out and couched his words more carefully. "I thought he needed space."

Irina saw right through him. "And back to my initial observation. This is more than a simple 'I do.'"

She wasn't wrong. "It's complicated," he hedged with a smile that grew wider when he thought about how simple it had become the past twenty-four hours, at least in some respects. Sure, everything about the situation was complicated—the case, their colleagues, David—but how Levi felt about Marsh? That part was simple. His chest still ached at the thought of moving on from Kristin, but she would have loved Marsh and wanted this for him and David. Would have laughed at Marsh's cockiness, at how fast he'd twisted Levi up, at how perfect a proposal it actually was. She'd be the first to raise her glass to them. Levi cleared his throat around the knot lodged there. "Stomach swooping was—is —definitively involved."

"In the good way?"

"Mostly good," he said. "As for his proposal, fancy

restaurant, bottle of champagne, told me to marry him before he told me his name."

Irina hooted and slapped a hand against the table, drawing everyone's attention. "Sounds about right, and judging by the smile you can't wipe off your face, I'd say things are on their way to uncomplicated."

Lily saved him from answering, impersonating Mama Nina and banging on the table, finally tipping Holt's soda all over her father. A dog's bark joined the cacophony of noise, and Levi whipped his head the direction of the new noise. Marsh and Camilla were returning, a stray cow and limping calf in tow. The noise around Levi faded, his attention solely focused on the man he'd been missing. Not even Marsh's obvious exhaustion—from the downward tilt of his chin to his slumped shoulders—could detract from Mount Cowboy in all his glory. He was impressive as hell on horseback, a natural. As if sensing the attention, Marsh lifted his face and locked eyes with Levi. Didn't look away like he had most of the day. Had the ride settled him? Would he let Levi give him what he needed? Did Levi stand a chance of convincing him how simple this could be?

"He's careful with you," Irina said.

"He is." Levi acknowledged their connection, the check-in with a nod to Marsh before turning back to Irina. "Even if he thinks he hasn't been."

"Whatever the story, he's invested in you and David." Levi recognized the tone and expression of a concerned parent. Liked her more for it. "Be careful with him too."

"Yes, ma'am."

As quickly as her stern face had appeared, it vanished, Irina wriggling her nose and shaking her head. "Never call me ma'am again. Ruins the fantasy."

"Fantasy?"

She winked, then shot him the same flirty smile she'd given Brax earlier. Levi's cheeks heated, and he barely resisted covering them with his hands.

Laughing, Irina rose from the table, rounded the end, and clasped his shoulder. "He always was a sucker for a man who blushes."

As she sauntered off toward the barn Marsh and Camilla had disappeared into, Levi remained at the table, spinning the ring around his finger, embracing the swooping sensation in his stomach. This was the good kind. The sort he needed to hold on to and channel when he talked with Marsh. Use it to convince his husband that by his side was exactly where Levi wanted to be.

THREE

MARSH CLOSED THE STABLE DOOR, securing the drowsy calf with its mother to rest and recover, to wait for its injury to heal. Marsh's own mother, however, was less patient. "Okay, mijo," she said. "I gave you that whole ride out, two ropes, the ride back, and Irina splinting that calf's sprain to sort what you want to say. Spill."

He was impressed she'd bitten her tongue so long, giving him the time he'd needed to settle back into the land and their routine. The ninety minutes he'd needed to get out of his head, a respite from the horror reel playing on repeat—Levi's terrified face when the deadly pieces had come together, the worried faces of Levi's family who'd been asked to trust a stranger, David's frank assessment and distrust at the airport, the cadre of assassins who'd infiltrated San Diego. Family, granted, but wildcards Marsh had little control over, a connection that could cost Levi his job, the very thing Marsh had promised to try to protect. But Levi had to be alive to have a job, and Marsh was doing a piss-poor job protecting his and David's lives.

"Fuck." He slumped against the stable door and scrubbed his hands over his face, up under the brim of his hat, and into his hair.

"Just spit it out," his mother said as she grabbed his hat and tossed it onto a workbench. "You'll feel better."

She was probably right, but how much could he share without endangering his mothers? Without betraying Levi's confidence and their partnership or what was left of it? "There's more than just a ring involved here."

"Like your heart." Irina handed him a broom. "I see the way you look at him."

He avoided her gaze by feigning rapt attention to sweeping under the exam table. "He's a good man, hard not to admire."

"But it's different this time," Camilla said.

"How's that?"

Irina grabbed the top of the broom handle above where Marsh's hands were white-knuckling the shaft. She waited for him to lift his gaze. "He looks at you the same way."

"Mama—"

"It's your business. We know," Camilla said. "We learned to stay out of it a long time ago."

He cringed, hating that he'd made them feel like they couldn't ask about his life, romantic or otherwise.

Camilla caught the reflex and looped an arm around his waist, fitting herself to his side. "We learned because of your work, but you've always played this"—she patted his chest, over his heart—"close to the vest too. Ever since Patrick."

"And that's okay," Irina added as she pried the broom from his grip. "We just want you to be happy, and the way you and Levi look at each other, it's different even than what you and Patrick had."

What he and Levi had was different from what Marsh had had with his first love. Marsh was different. Maybe it was his age, maybe it was years of getting his heart broken by men who couldn't or wouldn't return his love, maybe it was finally finding the right man. He wanted to believe the earnest look in Levi's eyes last night and in his words when he'd asked Marsh to stay and be his partner. The connection between them was deeper, more raw, more precious, and more in danger than ever. "You're not wrong," he conceded. "And I need you to help me protect that, protect them."

"Figured," Camilla replied. "When you called, you said you needed a safe place to lie low." Her eyes flicked the direction of the picnic tables, where they could hear Brax calling after Holt. "And you brought the cavalry."

"More coming tomorrow." The Madigans weren't the only call he'd made.

"Figured that too. We've got the space between the main house and the bunkhouse."

Irina moved about the surgical bay, putting away supplies. "Especially as it's just us through the holiday weekend."

"Security?"

"How do you think I tracked that calf?" his mom answered.

"Instinct."

"That and MillieMinder." She dug her phone out of her pocket and flashed the app he'd first designed in high school to track Irina's then-favorite horse, a particularly willful mare that fancied herself an escape artist. They'd continued to refine and scale the app—livestock tracking, crop and feedstock monitoring, property surveillance—until they'd gone public with it and made more money from it in one year than Jefferson Marshall had made in his entire sorry life. "And even if my instincts or MM are off, nature will alert us." She pointed at the skylights above and the ravens perched on the metal frames.

Marsh shook his head. "You still feed them?"

She looked at him like he was an idiot. "Of course. Security and pest control for a handful of peanuts a day. Can't beat that deal."

Marsh kissed the top of her head. "Fuck, I missed you."

She patted his chest, then moved out of his arms and into Irina's. "I bet by now your new husband is missing you too."

Marsh couldn't say for sure. Yes, the weird silence had eased once they'd driven under the ranch gate, had seemed to dissipate over introductions and getting Levi and David settled in, but Marsh didn't know the root cause of it, and that worried him. Levi had rarely held his words, and they'd only become more frequent, more fervent, the longer they'd been together, culminating in the crescendo that had pierced the darkness around Marsh just before the plane had taken off in San Diego. Had the sun set on those words? Or on Levi's words from last night, the words Marsh's heart had ached for so long to hear, his affections returned? Levi had seemed almost physically ill on the drive in. From the stress, from the nightmare of the past fifteen hours, from David's reaction and the memory of Kristin, from Marsh's mere presence? Maybe Levi didn't want to see him at all. But that didn't stop Marsh from missing him something fierce, the pinch in his chest more uncomfortable than the unknown that awaited him.

"You two good?" he asked his moms.

"Under control," Irina said.

"Make a list of whatever foodstuffs we need," Marsh said as he grabbed his hat and headed for the door. "I'll hit the store in the morning."

"Get some rest," Camilla said.

"And some ass," Irina added.

He paused over the threshold, chuckling, then turned and crossed back to his moms, hugging them tight. What else could he do with these two wonderful women who never failed to guide him, to make him laugh, to love him? "Thank you."

Irina patted one cheek. "You never have to thank us for taking care of you and yours."

Camilla kissed the other. "You and yours are ours. This is home too. Always will be."

It was a comfort he'd always had—didn't realize how much he'd missed—until his husband had given it to him again.

FOUR

INSIDE THE HOUSE, Marsh found Brax drying dishes at the kitchen island and Holt seated at the table, Marsh's and Levi's personal laptops open on either side of his own sticker-covered monster. That single machine, covered as it was in rainbows and clovers, golden bears, and half a dozen other Bay Area decals, when wielded by the hacker behind it, could take down entire empires. Marsh smiled on his way to the sink. "I thought I taught you to keep our tools nondescript."

"Talk to your niece."

"Helena gave her a pack of stickers for St. Patty's Day," Brax explained. "It's like a leprechaun threw up all over the place."

"Where is the tiny ginger princess?"

"Out like a light." Holt shifted his focus among computers, fingers flying across multiple keyboards. "We called it a day after the great soda waterfall of 2022."

"Is that what happened to your hideous Raptors shirt?" Marsh asked with all the scorn he could summon. Holt had swapped the purple-and-red team shirt for a gray Madigan Cold Storage one.

Brax held out a fist for Marsh to bump. "Good riddance."

"I heard that." Holt's grin belied the toothless snark.

Ditto Brax's grin, the two of them completely smitten with each other. Marsh felt a pang of longing for his own husband who wasn't in the room. "He's on a call with his sister," Brax said, reading him right. And helping out by tossing a hand towel his direction, a welcome distraction.

"Thank you again for jumping on things so fast," Marsh said as he grabbed a plate from the drying rack.

"You'd do the same."

"But I didn't there for a while." He'd never forgive himself for the months he'd gone AWOL on two people who meant the world to him.

"Now we know why." Brax paused long enough to draw Marsh's gaze. "You didn't have to shoulder Sophie's death and the aftermath of that attack alone."

"I wasn't."

"I'm glad you had Sean, but we're here too. Always."

Marsh nodded, unable to force words out around the lump in his throat. They finished drying dishes in comfortable silence, working like the efficient team they'd been in the service, finishing just as Holt shut the laptops. He and Brax joined him at the table. "Sit rep," Marsh said.

"You want to wait for Levi?" Holt asked.

"I'll fill him in unless we need to wait?" Holt shook his head, and Marsh started where he knew Levi would want to. "Matt? Gail?"

"Both still in the hospital under our twenty-four-seven protection."

"And according to Mel," Brax said, referring to his friend and business partner, "Matt's former partner is also on the scene and throwing his weight around. In our favor."

Marsh mentally traced the web of connections, landing on Agent Kim's stint in Boston and a certain other Bostonian he'd met in the San Francisco field office. "Cameron Byrne? The ASAC in San Francisco?"

"That's the one," Brax said. "He's a good agent and tight with Talley and the assistant director. They finagled it so he's acting SAC for San Diego."

Marsh whistled low. "That's some juice." But was it enough? "What about Kwan?"

"Harder to spring," Holt said. "But Helena's working on it."

"Takes some extra doing as it's a holiday weekend." Brax extended his long legs, relaxed in his chair, and draped an arm across the back of Holt's. "We're pulling every string we've got."

Marsh propped his elbows on the table and scrubbed his hands over his face, frustration and weariness settling heavy on his shoulders. "How many people's holidays"—lives—"did I ruin?"

"I've seen worse," Holt said with a shrug.

Marsh didn't doubt it, including a hellish Christmas Eve the three of them and Kwan had been lucky to survive, but even that memory was little comfort now, standing as he was at the center of the present storm. He raked his fingers through his hair and clasped his hands behind his neck. In the company of trusted friends, he put words to the nagging thought chirping in the back of his mind. "I should have left when I was going to. I had my bags packed. I was ready to go."

"But…" Brax prompted.

"He asked me to keep a promise."

"And keeping that promise saved my son's life. Mine too."

Gaze jerking up, Marsh's collided with Levi's fiery blue one across the room. His eyes shone with a conviction Marsh wished like hell he could reflect but which had deserted him right about the time David had walked through the front door that morning. Would Marsh ever get the nightmare image of David holding the rigged chess set out of his head?

"Your husband's a smart man," Brax said, momentarily interrupting the horror reel. He stood and clasped Marsh's shoulder. "Listen to him."

Beside him, Holt finished unhooking computer cables, then stood and scooped up his stickered travesty. "Those are clean." He jutted his chin at the remaining two laptops. "No holes, and the walls are tight. Stop doubting yourself." Holt had a good read on him too.

But he had no idea the significance of his words to Levi, who waited until Brax and Holt were gone to approach the table. "Clean clean?" He warily eyed his laptop. "Like browser history clean?"

"I had him test the firewalls I built and check for any malware or other intrusions." Marsh chanced a touch, loosely snagging Levi's closest hand and running his thumb over his wedding band. "As for your browser history, I wiped that clean three weeks ago while I waited for you to walk into that restaurant."

Levi's hand jerked in his. Marsh started to let go, to give

him space, only to have Levi curl his fingers tight around Marsh's. "What?"

"I never should have made that threat, and I should have apologized for doing so before now. I'm sorry."

"Thank you, but I knew by the end of our conversation that it was an empty threat. That's not who you are." Levi rounded the table and rested back against the edge, hands still joined, thighs bumping, the air between them feeling lighter than it had all day.

"You were so quiet on the drive out here," Marsh said. "I thought…"

"Thought what?"

"That you'd changed your mind. That you regretted asking me to stay, to keep my promise."

"I was trying not to puke."

"Puke?" If Levi had been that sick over today's events, why—how—was he holding Marsh's hand, smiling down at him in that soft way Marsh had been falling for since their wedding day?

"Altitude sickness."

Relief swept through Marsh, and he thanked God he was seated. If he'd been standing, his legs would've given out for sure. As it was, he canted forward and rested his head on their joined hands. "Shit, Bishop, I didn't even think—"

"Neither did I." Levi carded his fingers through Marsh's hair, soothing and coaxing like he'd done last night, and relief settled deeper into Marsh's bones. "We're in the fucking desert for fuck's sake."

Marsh chuckled. "An elevated one."

"I went to this training thing in Albuquerque once.

Never been sicker in my life. I must have blocked it from my mind."

Marsh propped his chin on their hands, examining his husband more closely. Good color, steady breaths, eyes bright, pupils what he'd expect in the soft glow of the rustic chandelier's light. "You seem better now."

"Irina gave me a Zofran. Kristin wasn't lying when she called it a miracle drug."

Marsh averted his gaze, relief replaced with recriminations. "I'm sorry. I should have noticed and put it together sooner."

Levi's fingers tightened in his hair and forced his gaze back up. "Do you know how many times you've apologized since this morning?" Levi didn't give him a chance to count. "Eight hundred and twelve."

Marsh raised his brows. There'd been a lot he had to apologize for, but he didn't think there'd been that many.

"Okay, more like twenty-three, and that's twenty-three times too many."

"I brought this to your doorstep."

"It would have found its way there anyway. At least I know who's knocking." He cupped Marsh's cheek, and Marsh couldn't resist nuzzling into the warmth. "And you were there to play action hero."

"Speaking of twenty-three, I've apparently aged, and I'm not a stunt man."

"What hurts?"

"Everything."

Chuckling, Levi pushed off the table and untangled their fingers. Marsh opened his mouth to protest but groaned instead as Levi's strong hands landed on his shoulders, digging into the aching muscles. He stepped close behind Marsh, adding heat to the blissful ministrations. "And yet you went out on a horse and roped cattle."

Marsh closed his eyes and tipped his head back against Levi's chest. "Tradition."

Peaceful, comfortable silence enveloped them, and Marsh never wanted the perfect moment to end. But Levi had other ideas. He flattened his hands and slid them down Marsh's chest, applying extra pressure as they toyed with the cotton over Marsh's sensitive nipples. Warm tempting breath pooled behind Marsh's ear, Levi's voice a low purr when he spoke. "It was sexy seeing the cowboy in action." He brushed his lips along Marsh's neck, and goose bumps pricked Marsh's skin. Made the prick in his pants stand up and take notice too.

He angled his neck, offering Levi better access. "I must smell like airplane and horse."

"Fancy airplane, and I don't mind the cowboy part." He licked a stripe up Marsh's throat and nipped at his earlobe. Marsh jolted forward in the chair, Levi's arms over his shoulders barely keeping him seated. "A shower would probably ease some of your aches."

Lots of them, especially the increasingly urgent one behind his fly, but was Levi really ready to go there with him again after everything today? Marsh still couldn't believe it. "Are you sure you don't need more time? To process? To be sure?" Levi's lips on his, hard and fast, with the same conviction as his earlier gaze, answered Marsh's questions. Levi didn't need more time, but he did deserve a warning about what might come after the good parts tonight. "I'm probably not going to be good company after. If you do want to sleep in the loft or in one of the other rooms, I'll understand." As much as Marsh wanted to fall asleep with Levi in his arms, he'd understand if Levi actually wanted to sleep. "After Sophie died, after that explosion, it was weeks—"

"PTSD?"

Marsh nodded. "Twenty years in the army, more than a few explosions, including the one that almost killed Holt and Brax. We avoided the explosion this time"—he gestured with a hand near his head—"but my brain still went there."

Levi caught it, used it to tug him up and out of the chair. "I don't think I'm going to sleep much tonight either." He framed Marsh's face, thumbs pressing his lips shut, silencing any further protest. "But we'll worry about that later, after I give you what you need."

FIVE

LEVI SHUT the bedroom door and leaned back against it, admiring the room he and Marsh were sharing. Centered on one wall was a large king-size bed, the headboard and footboard hand carved, the nightstands on either side a matched set. Floor-to-ceiling windows spanned the length of the opposite wall, offering a magnificent view of Cathedral Mountain, the rocky top shining in the moonlight. Directly across from Levi, on the other side of the bed, was a chest of drawers and the door to the bathroom Marsh had disappeared into. As for the wall Levi stood against, it was a riot of color, a painted field of sunflowers—bright yellow, vivid green, and rich brown—that climbed all the way to the loft above. The sheer number of flowers was impossible to count, their vibrancy impossible to describe. "What's the story behind this one?" he asked when Marsh emerged from the bathroom. He'd learned earlier about the murals in the living room and kitchen. He was sure the story behind this one would be good too.

"Amor Anter," Marsh said as he dug through his duffel

atop the dresser. "After the Cold War ended, once it was safe to go back, Irina's father took her to Poland. Amor Anter is the sunflower that's farmed in the town where her family is from."

"Do they grow here?" It would be hard to capture such vibrance, such life, from a photo or memory. Levi would bet the artist, the brother of the man who'd designed his and Marsh's rings, had seen these in person.

Marsh jerked free his toiletry kit and threw a cryptic smile over his shoulder, his only answer before vanishing back into the bathroom.

Levi wanted to chase after that grin and its owner, but he needed to be sure someone else was settled first. He cracked open the door and listened for any sounds from David's room down the hall. Hearing none, he closed the door with a quiet snick, locked it, then scurried around the end of the bed, shedding clothes as he went. Down to his boxers, he leaned a bare shoulder against the bathroom doorjamb and looked his fill at the shirtless mountain of a cowboy at the vanity. And mentally thanked Camilla and Irina for their foresight. "Your moms are clever."

"Some would say too clever." Marsh straightened from over the sink and lowered the washcloth from his face. Catching sight of Levi in the mirror, his breath hitched, and his darkening gaze raked over him from head to toe, leaving a fiery trail of heat in its wake. "But if you're refer-ring to the fact there's an empty room and bathroom between us and David, then yes, that's Thelma and Louise being clever."

Levi chuckled, the description apt. Everything had been so topsy-turvy when they'd arrived, his list of worries already so long that Levi hadn't added sleeping arrangements to it. At the time, he'd just been happy there was an en suite bath so if he needed to puke, he could do so in private. Thankfully, it hadn't come to that, and now, with his stomach and heart more settled, he appreciated that he and Marsh were in the same wing as David but at the end of the hall with empty rooms between them. And with a lofted bed above, in case David had objected to him and Marsh sharing a room, which he hadn't. He was too busy with the tablet full of chess sims Holt had lent him, channeling his energy there while he continued to process everything that had happened. David had burned through his initial anger, which was good, but Levi knew his son. There'd be more, plus a firestorm of anxiety and questions, including about where things were going with him and Marsh. But those were conversations for tomorrow, after rest and after Levi took care of the person who'd taken care of them, who'd kept them safe.

"Now, about that shower." Levi pushed off the jamb, barely resisted the acres of bronze skin on display, and reached around the half wall into the stone enclave, flipping on the water. He quickly reversed, aiming to avoid the initial blast of cold, and ran into a wall of heat against his back, Marsh caging him in.

"Last out."

The two rough syllables vibrated up Levi's spine, sparking flames that warmed Levi to his core, chasing away any lingering chill. "I don't want a fucking out." Marsh all around him was Levi's new favorite state of being. The only thing better was Marsh inside him. He rocked his hips, his ass teasing Marsh's stiffening erection. "I want you."

One hand left on the pony wall, a small bottle beneath his palm, Marsh skated his other hand down Levi's side.

Rough pressure scraped over Levi's nerve endings, lighting more fires that roared to an inferno when Marsh shoved his hand inside his boxers and palmed his ass. Levi shot out his arms, catching himself on the wall for balance, then rocked harder into Marsh, greedy for more of his touch, for more of that delicious heat. Marsh gave it to him, yanking down his boxers, spreading his ass cheeks, and notching his denim-clad erection right where Levi wanted it. The opposite of gentle and everything Levi needed. He rotated his hips and keened, loving the friction and loving Marsh's responsiveness, his husband coming back to life after a day spent shut down.

Snaking an arm under his, Marsh splayed a hand on his chest, forced Levi upright, and breathed heated words into his ear. "Do you have any idea what you do to me?"

Levi cradled his own erect cock, showing Marsh just how hard he was for him too. "Yeah, baby, I think I do."

Marsh groaned and sank against him, pinning Levi to the wall, Levi's arm trapped between body and stone. Which thank fuck because Marsh's tortured, "Fuck, I need…" almost made Levi explode. A firm grip on his balls was all that saved him.

"What do you need?" He'd give Marsh anything—everything—if he would just give Levi his lips and his cock. Give him the intimacy and connection he craved after almost losing it all. "Tell me."

Marsh buried his face in the crook of his neck, uncharacteristically silent, hesitating to even ask for what he wanted much less tell him. But his body betrayed him, rutting hips and straining erection giving away his desire. He wanted Levi as much as Levi wanted him, but he didn't believe his affections were returned. That he was worthy of it.

Using all his strength, Levi pushed off the wall, forcing Marsh back and creating enough space to rotate. He coasted his hands up sweat-dappled skin, through the light smattering of Marsh's chest hair and higher to frame his downturned face. "Look at me."

Marsh lifted his chin.

Oh.

His dark eyes swirled with the emotions Levi expected —desire warring with doubt—but he didn't expect the combination, the honesty and vulnerability in exposing the battle, to be so damn sexy. Knees weak, Levi used the shower wall to hold him up as he dragged Marsh closer. He brushed their lips together, a promise before spilling all his conviction into words. "My son is safe under this roof because of you. You gave me what I need. Now let me give you what you need."

Marsh held his gaze for the longest ten seconds of Levi's life, then withdrew his other hand from the shower wall and planted it in the center of Levi's chest, forcing Levi to grab the bottle. "Make sure you take that into the shower."

Levi glanced down at the tube in his hand. And laughed out loud. Only Emmitt Marshall could both claim him and surrender to him with a bottle of lube.

Marsh hitched one side of his mouth, a hint of a smirk, as he removed the rest of his clothes. "Something funny, Bishop?"

Levi would have done a victory dance if he'd had more room. He settled for a slow roll off the wall, intentionally bringing as much of his naked body into contact with the hard one revealed in front of him. "Just my husband." Taking Marsh's hand in his, he led him into the shower, tossed the lube onto the stone bench, and guided Marsh under the showerhead. Tension melted away in the steam and hot water, Levi helping the relaxation along by kneading Marsh's neck and shoulders, by lightly scratching his back, by running his soapy hands through the thick mop of black hair. Marsh leaned against him for a change, his big body loose and pliant, except for his erection. Levi's was likewise begging for attention, streaking Marsh's backside with precome. Marsh didn't seem to mind, occasionally reaching back to hold Levi closer, by his hip or cock, languidly stroking as his head lolled on Levi's shoulder.

As much as Levi enjoyed the lazy, intimate minutes, wouldn't mind countless more of them, neither their bodies nor sleep would wait forever. He finished rinsing the suds from Marsh's hair, sloughed the soap bubbles off his body, then circled around to his front and pushed Marsh back a step, making room for himself to wash in the fall of water. With intention and in view. Allowing Marsh to stare at the exposed column of his neck, to witness his nipples hardening as Levi passed the washcloth over them, to see for himself the heavy weight of Levi's cock and balls as he soaped them, the flex of muscle, the waiting hole as he rinsed his ass. By the time Levi was done and tossed his rag onto the bench seat, Marsh could have been generating his own steam, his limbs practically vibrating, his dark eyes smoldering.

Levi closed the distance between them and pressed their bodies together, their cocks rutting as neither he nor Marsh could resist rolling their hips, the promised friction too tempting. "Tell me what you need."

Marsh cradled his face, gentle yet firm, and skated a thumb over his lips. "To kiss you until these lips are bruised and swollen."

Levi lunged, slamming their mouths together. He was done with teasing. He needed the force and urgency of Marsh attacking his mouth, of Marsh forcing his tongue between his lips and claiming every secret space inside him, starting there. Stolen gasps between greedy sucks and nips. When they finally came up for air, Levi was pinned against the shower wall, his lips tingling. Other parts of him aching. He held Marsh close, one arm around his waist, the other over his shoulder. "What do you need next?"

Marsh's gaze remained fixed on his lips. "To see those swollen lips stretched around my cock." Levi started for his knees, but Marsh stopped him, jutting his chin at the shower ledge instead. "Sit there." Levi sat with his ass on the edge of the stone bench. Marsh kicked his legs farther apart, spreading him wide. "Need to see how hard you are for me." He stepped between Levi's spread legs, planted his hands on the wall over his head, and thrust his hips forward, offering Levi more of what he needed too.

Canting forward, Levi clasped Marsh's thighs and nosed the underside of his cock. He swirled his tongue around the base, around his balls, everywhere but where a cursing Marsh wanted it. Fingers plowed into his hair, curled around the wet strands, and tilted back his head, the searing sting all pleasure, no pain. "Around my cock," Marsh gritted out, sounding like he was barely hanging on.

Levi couldn't stop the smile that stretched across his face. Marsh's eye roll made him smile wider. He was still smiling as his lips parted around the tip of Marsh's cock, taking just the head inside his mouth before he pulled back to circle the tip with his tongue. He repeated the motion again and again, a little farther down Marsh's cock each time, until finally he took Marsh to the back of his throat and swallowed. Above him, Marsh growled and slapped the shower wall. Levi drew back slowly, tongue flattened along the underside of Marsh's cock the entire way, intending to start the torture over again, but Marsh demanded more, punching his hips forward. Levi gave it to him, sucking in earnest, groaning as Marsh used him, tested his limits, covered his tongue in tangy precome. He was coming undone, and Levi was more turned on than ever. He reached a hand between his legs to grasp his cock, to stroke some of the ache away, but Marsh tightened the hand still in his hair, pulling him off his cock. He stepped back and offered Levi a hand up.

Levi stood, admiring his husband's thrumming body. "What do you need now?"

Hand to his hip, Marsh reached around him and plucked the bottle of lube off the bench. Straightening, he rotated Levi to face the shower wall, adjusted his position so his ass wasn't in the spray of water, then dribbled lube down Levi's crack. Marsh's hand followed, fingers on a direct path to his hole, a finger circling and pushing in, Marsh stretched over his back. "To make you come so hard you have to muffle your screams so everyone in this house doesn't hear you."

Levi punched his hips back. "Fuck yes." He rode Marsh's finger, then two, then three, as Marsh worked him open. "Harder," he pleaded. "More," he begged on repeat until Marsh gave them both what they needed, his cock buried balls-deep inside Levi. It was Levi's turn to slap the wall, Marsh's slow, long strokes perfect torture. Made even more so when Marsh grasped the underside of his knee, hitched his leg up, and placed his foot on the bench, opening him wider, penetrating him deeper, hurling him closer to the edge as he wrapped a lube-slick hand around Levi's cock, stroking in rhythm with his thrusts.

Levi was on the verge, the threatened scream right there, and panic rushed up. He looked around frantically. What the fuck could he use to muffle the release barreling down on him? Marsh gave him the answer, offered him what he needed, three fingers pressed against his swollen lips. Levi opened his mouth and sucked them in, groaned around them, as Marsh poured pleasure into him, pumping through his orgasm, then wringing Levi's from him, stroking his cock until he covered Marsh's hand and the shower wall with his come.

Marsh slipped his fingers from his mouth, but Levi grasped his wrist before he could go far, holding his hand over his chest, the two of them panting and resting together against the shower wall. "Do you need anything else?"

Marsh turned off the water, then looped his arm around Levi's waist, his forehead against Levi's nape. "To fall asleep with you in my arms where I know you're safe."

The very thing Levi needed too.

SIX

MARSH WAS PICKING clothes up off the floor and folding them on the end of the dresser when Levi snuck back into the bedroom, quietly closing the door behind him. "He good?" Marsh asked after David.

"Fell asleep playing chess." Levi's soft smile was firmly in place, a gravitational force that drew Marsh to his side.

He hauled Levi into his arms, his skin still warm beneath the tee and sweats he'd thrown on, his damp hair a fascinating mix of brown and blond, the strands drying unevenly. Marsh pushed a few off his forehead, then cupped the back of Levi's neck, holding him gently to his chest. Safe and sound. "Is he good?" Marsh asked again, not just about David's current state but overall.

"Tomorrow will be rough," Levi said, grasping the subtle distinction. "Right now, there's just a lot. We'll see if he sleeps and how surly he is in the morning."

"It's July Fourth weekend. Plenty of distraction if he needs it."

"Good, we can use that."

They stayed wrapped in each other's arms for several minutes, the sort of peace and contentment that had been missing from Marsh's life before Levi. He wasn't the least bit embarrassed about his grumble when Levi eventually stepped away. Did even less to hide his groan as Levi shucked out of his pants and shirt, miles of taut muscle and freckled skin on moonlit display before he burrowed under the covers.

Marsh wanted to tuck in with him more than anything in the world right then, but if David woke and came looking for Levi, or if Marsh tossed and turned all night… He'd already gotten more than he'd hoped for tonight; he shouldn't ask for more. He flicked his gaze to the loft above. "There's a bed up there or another room on the other side of David's. I can—"

Levi patted the mattress next to him. "You said you needed me here tonight. With you."

"I do." A few minutes in each other's arms wasn't enough. "But only if you're good with it."

He held up the covers. "More than."

Marsh was a little embarrassed at how fast he dove under the covers, but Levi's quiet laughter was worth it. So was stretching out alongside his warm body. "You know what else was more than?"

Levi carded his fingers through his hair. "What's that?"

"Sex with you in the shower."

"Was that a fantasy of yours?" he asked, a sexy satisfied grin in his voice.

"What do you think happened after I got you off that night in the kitchen?" He smoothed a hand across Levi's chest, then gave his nipple a twist. Served him right for being smug. "I barely made it to the shower before I blew."

"Why did you leave that night?"

"Because that night was about giving you the release you needed." He rested his hand over Levi's heart, the moonlight through the windows glinting off his wedding band. "You weren't ready for this—for us—yet. I can't help but wonder…"

"If I am now?" Levi snuck a finger under his chin and lifted it, forcing his gaze. Marsh expected frustration or confusion, maybe a touch of anger. All that stared back at him was genuine curiosity. "Why do you think that?"

"You're still grieving. The last thing I want to do is rush you." If Marsh ever wanted this to be real, which he did—desperately—it had to proceed on a timeline that worked for both of them.

"I'll always be grieving," Levi said with a sad but accepting smile. "I lost a wonderful partner, my best friend, the mother of my child, but there's nothing I can do to bring her back. Living in the past won't honor her memory. She'd want me to move on, to be happy. That's how I'll honor her. That's how I'll set an example for our son."

Marsh planted a forearm on the mattress and levered up, kissing his husband, one of the best men he'd ever known. "You're something special, Levi Bishop."

Levi smiled and shifted them to their sides so they were lying face to face. "I won't lie and say fits of guilt won't strike. Those moments will happen, and you—" He shook Marsh's shoulder. "You have to not freak out or think I'm pushing you away."

"We've all got our ghosts."

"I feel like yours may be scarier than mine."

"I was serious before. I'm probably not going to sleep much tonight. If I start to dream—"

"Don't wake you up. My dad gave us that talk."

He was too perfect a fit, inviting him into his world, ghosts and all.

Into his family, which wasn't unaffected by all this.

"Speaking of family, what did Amy have to say earlier?"

"Mom and Aunt Liz are still speaking, so let's call that a win."

A major one from all Marsh had heard.

"You debriefed with Holt and Brax?" Levi asked, and Marsh nodded. "Matt, Gail, and Kwan?"

"Helena, that's Holt's sister, the blond at the airport." He waited for Levi's nod, letting him connect the dots before continuing. "She's the best defense attorney I know. She's representing Kwan."

"I wouldn't have pegged her for an attorney."

Good instincts. "That's not all she does." Good instincts again by not asking for more details. Marsh carried on. "She's doing what she can to get the charges dismissed before the arraignment Tuesday, but the holiday makes it tough."

"Fuck." Levi ran a hand through his hair, pushing back the strands that had crept forward again. "Matt and Gail?"

"Gail has been discharged with a guard. As for Matt…" He rolled out of Levi's arms to snag his phone off the night-stand. He opened the latest encrypted email from Holt, a forwarded voice recording from Byrne. "This came through while you were checking on David. Hit Play."

"Planes! All I really want is planes! In the morning, planes! In the evening, planes!" As off-key as it was, the Beastie Boys melody was unmistakable as was Matt's New York accent.

Levi stifled his laugh in a pillow. "He hates the jets from

Miramar," he said between guffaws. "And he's high as a kite obviously."

"Docs are giving him the good drugs." Marsh tossed the phone back on the table, then rolled to face Levi again. "He's also got an ASAC watching over him. Cameron Byrne, his old partner from Boston."

"He's the ASAC in San Francisco, right? I met him last December."

Marsh nodded. "Our bases are covered. Or as covered as they can be for now."

"I'll take it." Levi cuddled closer, head tucked under his chin, arm over his waist, leg wedged between his. Still so unbelievable.

"Are you sure about this, Levi? I know what you said earlier. I know I said 'last out,' but—"

"The last three weeks have been a whirlwind, but they've also been the best, most normal three weeks in two years." Levi angled his face and kissed the underside of Marsh's chin. "You delivered on everything you promised. Stability, my case solved, a partner at work and home. Now it's my turn to do the same."

"You don't have to."

"I want to." He snuggled closer, and Marsh drew the blanket his grandmother had quilted over them. "I want these assholes behind bars. I want to see justice served for their victims, including Sophie. I want to keep working with you, and I want to see where this goes. Romantic chess and all that."

Marsh chuckled. "Romantic chess? Do you even know what that is?"

Levi shrugged, his reply slurred with encroaching sleep.

"I'll just throw around the term and pretend I know what I'm doing."

"You've got the bold moves down but no sacrifices." Marsh dropped a kiss on his head, his own eyelids heavy, the long day and roller coaster of emotions catching up to him. "Not without talking to me first."

Levi's light snores were his only reply.

SEVEN

THE LOW HUM of muted voices and the warmth of sunlight nudged Levi toward waking. The heat was comfortable and tempted him to stay in bed as it filtered through the gauzy curtains he'd pulled over the windows last night during one of his many trips down the hall to check on David. Either he'd wake from the nightmare where Marsh didn't get to David in time—or Marsh would wake, from Levi guessed, a similar hell—and he'd need to make sure his son was safe and sound, not blown to bits. David had slept through the night; he and Marsh, not so much. Marsh must have given up at some point earlier in the morning, his side of the bed cool, his drawl among the voices outside. Giving up himself, Levi flopped onto his back and let the mattress, the soft sheets, his sore ass, and the lingering scent of his husband provide a fleeting moment of peace to add to his severely depleted well.

His brain, however, once awake, refused to rest. He was putting together mental to-do lists before he could stop himself—the list of people he needed to check on, the tasks he and Marsh needed to tackle to connect the chessboard attacks to Eder Capital, phase two—

The bedroom door swung open—no knock, no warning —and David darted inside. Just as quickly, he shut the door behind him, barely avoiding a slam. Levi wondered who his son was running from. Or hiding from.

David spun on his heel, caught sight of Levi's no doubt epic bed head and the love bites on his chest, then, with the wide-eyed look of a horrified teen, spun right back around like he wanted to run the opposite direction but had no way out. He settled for banging his forehead on the door. "OMG, can this morning get any more awkward?"

Chuckling, Levi scooted to the end of the bed and leaned over the side. "How'd it get awkward to start?" He snagged his sweats, yanked them on, then stood. Nausea and wooziness hit him like a crashing wave, forcing him to grab a bedpost for balance.

David thankfully didn't notice, too caught up in his own crisis. Still facing the door, he flung an arm out behind him, pointing in the direction of the backyard. "The hottest man I've ever seen in my life is out there."

"Roger Moore?"

David flipped his hand and shot him the bird.

"Gotta be Marsh." The answer was a no-brainer to Levi, and God forgive him, he couldn't help needling David a bit more when he was this deep into his drama.

He made a retching sound and violently shook his head. "Gross, my stepdad, no!"

"Holt or Brax?"

Shook his head again.

One of the new voices, then. Levi could swear he'd heard them before but couldn't quite place them. The voice with the hint of Midwest was cultured in that family money sort of way. The other one was an odd sort of Southern-British hybrid, slow like molasses, drawling, but with a touch of the Queen's English.

"Don't get me wrong," David carried on as Levi wobbled his way to the bathroom, using the furniture and walls to stay upright. "Marsh is hot and all, but he's my stepdad, and he's old, so no."

"Hey!" Levi shouted around his toothbrush. "He's not that much older than me." He finished brushing, washed his face, pulled on a tee, and downed the Zofran waiting for him on the vanity.

"Brax is even older, and Holt…" David sighed. "Fine, he's hot in that bad-boy, teddy-bear way, but two gingers rarely make a right."

"You know you just sealed your fate." Levi crossed the room back to the bed and situated himself against the headboard. "You can turn around now. Your delicate eyeballs are safe."

David did so with his hands over his face, peeking through his fingers.

Levi threw a pillow at him. "So who's the hot one?"

Catching the pillow, David crashed onto the other side of the bed. "He's not as bulky as Holt, which is fine with me, and his eyes and hair are just…" He flopped onto his back, arm over his face, and Levi had to cover his mouth to stifle a laugh. It had been a long time since he'd seen David this animated. This was like the before times when he and Kristin used to wind each other up or join forces to wind up Levi. "I didn't think I liked man buns but… ngh…" He rolled back over, burying his flaming red face in the pillow.

Levi ruffled his hair. "Name, David."

He mumbled into the pillow. "Trevor something-hyphen last name."

Ah, now Levi put it together. The name, the accent, the pictures Marsh had shown him. "Trevor Caldwell-Henby? Sean's husband?" Which meant the Midwest voice was Sean Henby-Paxton's, Marsh's former legat colleague and other best friend. Sean had left the FBI last year to marry Trevor and Charlie, his college sweethearts, and to run his family's empire after his adopted father's death.

David heaved another sigh, lifted his face from the pillow, and propped an elbow on it. "And what even is that accent? I've never heard anything like it."

"Coastal North Carolina." Now that he knew who it was, Levi could place the accent. "A buddy of mine at the Academy used to call it High Tider."

But David wasn't actually interested in answers. He collapsed back on the pillow. "And of course his wife is gorgeous too. And all commanding and shit. I've never been attracted to women, but she turned my head."

"Charlie's here too?"

"Yeah, they got here this morning. And their husband's hot too in a boy-next-door way. How is that even pos—" He stopped midsentence, turned his nose to the pillow again, and sniffed. "Marsh slept here?" He flicked his gaze to the loft above. "Not up there?"

Levi patted the bed next to him. "We need to talk."

David looked back and forth between him and the pillow. "So the night before last…" His face and shoulders fell. "Fuck, that feels like a lifetime ago."

Levi didn't bother correcting his language. They had more important things to discuss than words that were arbitrarily deemed rude. "David, come here."

He dragged himself upright and leaned against the headboard. Levi threw an arm around his shoulders and hugged him to his side. "You sleep okay?"

"Like shit."

"You were out when I checked on you."

"I pretended to be asleep whenever you or Marsh poked your heads in." Levi's heart warmed at the consideration both men had shown him, but the happy vibes were tempered by worrisome ones as David deflated, his earlier burst of energy depleted, which made sense if he hadn't slept a wink either. "Every time I heard a noise, I thought someone was trying to break in and get to you. And it's the country out there." He gestured at the windows, then let his hand flop to his lap and his head onto Levi's shoulder. "So many noises."

"Marsh's moms have an app that monitors the farm, including security. I'll ask Marsh to download it to your burner." He rubbed David's outer shoulder, waiting for him to lift his gaze. "But David, I think we're safe here."

"I thought we were safe at home. I can't lose you too."

What little peace Levi had summoned vanished, the worry fully eclipsing any happy. "I'm sorry—"

"Don't be." David averted his gaze and wrung his hands. "I'm the idiot who left the chess set on the patio table and didn't notice it was heavier when I picked it up off the porch."

Levi and Marsh had learned those facts at the scene. "Like I told you yesterday, I would rather someone steal it from outside our house than inside. And as for the weight, it was an easy mistake. You weren't the only one who made it."

David seemed to contemplate that, silent once more as

he leaned against Levi, the muffled voices outside the only noise. Until he spoke again, so quiet and timid he hardly seemed like the same excited teen from five minutes ago. "Do you love him?"

"I've known him for three weeks. I can't say that. *Yet.*" David blew out a long breath, then sucked it back in as Levi continued. "But what I can say is that he's made a positive impact on our lives."

"Nonna's lasagna makes a positive impact."

"Don't be a wanker."

"Hey!"

There was the surly teen Levi knew and loved. Levi ruffled his hair, and David's scowl deepened. Levi didn't think the truth he had to tell him was going to make the frown any better, but he owed David that. And had promised Kristin. "Truth?"

David hesitated, but after a hard swallow, he lifted his gaze and nodded. Jesus, Levi loved his kid. Twenty-four hours of hell and David was still chin up, ready to accept more change in his life. For all his grumpiness, he was one of the bravest people Levi knew. And one of his favorites. Levi should have never doubted him.

"I like him a lot," he told David. "I like how he fits with us, how he's made us both laugh, and how well we all work together."

"It's not like Mom." His tone wasn't defensive, more like a statement of fact.

Which Levi didn't dispute. "No one will ever be like Kristin. She was one of a kind. And she was your mom."

"Okay." David picked up Marsh's pillow and handed it to Levi. "And I get what you're saying. Things have been better with Marsh around."

Levi crossed his legs, plopped the pillow in his lap, and rested his elbows on it. "If it ever stops being better, I need you to tell me. You have to be on board with wherever things between me and Marsh go. As much as I want to stick my face in this pillow—"

"Eww, gross, Dad!"

Laughing, he tossed the pillow aside. "Okay, but seriously"—he waited for David to meet his eyes a final time—"I won't make myself happy at your expense. Period."

"Okay, I can live with that, on one condition."

"What's that?"

He patted his stomach. "Marsh makes that breakfast casserole at least once a week."

Always the bottomless pit. "I think that can be arranged," he said with a laugh before swinging his legs over the side of the bed and standing. Feeling steadier inside and out, he met his son at the end of the bed. "Now, let me finish cleaning up, and then we'll go see this new crush of yours."

"Prepare yourself."

EIGHT

DAVID WAS RIGHT, and Levi was unprepared. Hotness overload had invaded Mi Herencia. The pictures Marsh had shown him of the Caldwell-Henby-Paxton clan did not do the trio justice. Charlotte was beautiful—dark hair, dark eyes, legs for days, but as David had rightly observed, it was her bearing and command of the room that was most striking. A natural leader and clearly the throuple's center, both men gravitating around her. Trevor was equally beautiful, though Levi would rank the easy smile and hazel eyes over the man bun that so fascinated David. But neither Charlie nor Trevor were as fascinating to Levi as Sean was. He seemed the opposite of Marsh in almost every way. His size and build were closer to Levi's—if a bit smaller—his features were strong yet refined, and his clean-cut and casual style exuded both wealth and down-to-earth vibes. He was a mess of contradictions. Maybe that was what had intrigued Marsh. Or maybe it was just Sean's classic good looks—dark hair, blue eyes, full lips.

David elbowed his side. "Your husband is there." He

pointed at Marsh, who was seated at the picnic table with Lily on his hip, the trio standing behind him chatting with Holt and Brax.

Marsh lifted his mug in greeting. "It's a lot. I know." He smirked as he plucked a doughnut from a pink pastry box on the table. Lily promptly stole it, so he snagged another. "I showed up in Hanover last year, saw all three of them together, and nearly combusted."

Sean smacked his shoulder. "Stop lying. You swaggered into the station house and flirted with everyone in sight." Okay, so maybe that's why Marsh liked him; Sean just got him. The former legat turned business executive shifted his attention to Levi, hand extended. "Sean Henby-Paxton. It's great to meet you, Levi." His smile was somehow practiced and genuine, leaning more into the latter as he introduced his partners. "This is my wife, Charlie, and our husband, Trevor."

Charlie's smile was warm and inviting, the dash of mischief in her eyes making her even more attractive. "You okay with a hug?" she asked, her High Tider accent like-wise strong. "We're from the South, we hug, and you're family now."

"Hugs it is," Levi said with open arms, embracing Charlie, then Trevor before Sean snuck in for the tightest hug of all.

"Thank you," Sean whispered before pulling away. Levi didn't have to ask what for. Even if Marsh didn't realize how special he was to his friends, how much they wanted happiness for him too, Levi recognized it and was thankful Marsh had friends like that in his life. And now so did he and David, who he nudged forward. "This is my son, David." They hugged him too, David turning bright red, but Sean got him talking, easily drawing him into conversation about the ranch. The guy would have made one hell of a politician, but to hear Marsh tell it, Sean would rather give politicians hell than ever be one himself.

"David, Trevor," Irina interrupted as she and Camilla strode toward them. "You can hit the vet rounds with me or ride out with Camilla and Lily."

Trevor leaned close to David and whispered conspiratorially, "This is the *we're not supposed to hear it* portion of the morning."

A grinning Trevor stole David's words.

Charlie whispered conspiratorially to Levi. "There's a reason he's the most popular professor in the lit department at Georgetown, and it's got nothing to do with Shakespeare."

"I'm gonna have to skip the vet rounds," Trevor said to Irina with an apologetic smile. "I'm a hard pass on needles."

David all of a sudden found his words again. Shocker that. "I'd like to see the ranch. Marsh talks a lot about it." Levi didn't think that's all he wanted to see. But there was apparently a tiny part of his brain not thinking about the sexy lit professor. "Can I do vet rounds with you tomorrow?" he asked Irina. "It's something I'm interested in," David added, surprising Levi. Yes, things had improved at home, David engaging more, Marsh drawing them both back into the world of the living, but the hard work of reconnecting had just begun. He needed more time with David; it was part of the reason he'd agreed to Marsh's proposal in the first place. Time was tight, and they needed to start having conversations with David about his future.

"Of course," Irina said. "The work never stops."

"Horses!" Lily chimed in excitedly around her last bite of doughnut.

"Which one are you gonna ride?" Marsh asked. "Penelope or Luther? Or maybe Buck?"

Camilla plucked Lily off his lap. "You're riding with me, carina."

Lily clapped. "Buck!"

"Mom's horse," Marsh said.

Though Levi was behind a step, caught midshiver. "Lily can ride?"

"I wish he'd never put her on a horse," Holt said, similarly apprehensive. "But here we are. It's all she wants to do."

Marsh tickled the bottom of his niece's bare foot. "She takes after her uncle." She giggled, squirmed out of Camilla's arms, and ran toward the barn.

"Shoes!" Holt called after his daughter.

"I best catch up before she tries to ride by herself." She pecked Marsh's upturned cheek, Irina's lips, then hustled after the tiny ginger terror, David and Trevor in their wake.

"Sunscreen!" Levi shouted after his son, though he didn't think it would do much for his son's beet red skin, especially not following Trevor around on a horse all day.

"Should we take this inside?" Brax said once the civilians were out of earshot. "Some place it's not on the way to eighty billion degrees."

"You spent twenty years in the desert," Marsh countered.

"Yes, but I'm not from it like you or Levi. I prefer the fog."

Holt looped an arm around his waist. "That's my man."

"Fine," Marsh said, pushing to his feet. "I could use

more coffee. My body thinks it's five in the morning." He reached Levi's side and wrapped an arm around him, same as Holt had done. "And there's tea for you too. Ginger kind to help your stomach."

Good, because judging by Charlie's determined stride, by Holt and Brax with their heads together, by Sean's pensive look, reflected on Marsh's face too, another long roller coaster day was just beginning.

NINE

MARSH DIDN'T WANT to lean too heavily on Levi. He wasn't as green as he'd been yesterday, but Marsh had noticed his deeper breathing and his slower steps each time he'd gotten up last night to check on David. He must have taken the Zofran this morning, which had restored enough balance to shower and make his way outside, but the fact he didn't immediately go for tea or a doughnut betrayed his queasiness. While the strategy session ahead would likely lead to frustration, at least it would take Levi's mind off the altitude sickness for a spell.

Once inside, Marsh directed his husband toward the stone hearth that separated the living area from the kitchen. This time of morning, it would still be cool, the sun on the other side of the house. He ducked into the kitchen for Levi's tea, a refill of his coffee, then claimed the spot beside Levi. Across from them, Charlie perched on the arm of the couch, Sean on the cushion beside her, while Holt, with his laptop, sank into the living room chair next to the one Brax had chosen.

"Has our mess gotten back to Washington?" Marsh asked Charlie. While serving as deputy chief of police in Hanover, she'd nailed the cartel that had killed her brother and father. That had put her on the FBI's radar, and she'd been recruited to the organized crimes division and relocated to DC, where Sean's family's company, Paxton Industries, was now headquartered.

"You could say that." Charlie crossed one jean-clad leg over the other. "And it's locked down tight. My SAC tried to wrangle the case, given the connections to organized crime, domestic and international."

"And because her SAC worked with Agent Kwan in New York," Sean added. "As soon as he'd heard she'd been arrested, he called bullshit."

Kwan's impeccable reputation and skillfully built network were paying off, but Marsh was sensing a caveat. He parsed Charlie's words. Her boss had *tried* and by her tone, *failed* to wrangle the case. "But…"

"Representative Anthony showed up and demanded all of it be shut down," Charlie said. "Immediately."

It was a good thing Marsh had his hand on Levi's thigh. He suspected it was the only thing that kept Levi seated. As it was, he jolted hard enough to slosh tea over the rim of his cup. "On what grounds?"

"According to Anthony, per your late SAC, your"—she pointed at Levi—"case is solved, you"—she pointed at Marsh—"interfered, and Eder Capital is not the FBI's problem."

Levi set aside his cup, then ticked off the counterarguments on his fingers, needing both hands. "We have two missing persons, a dead SAC who was in a politician's pocket, four attempted murders, three of those federal agents, a bitcoin money laundering scheme, human trafficking, identity theft and digital forgery, and what the fuck do we have legats for if Eder Capital isn't our business?"

"Don't forget the fugitive facilitator," Marsh added to the list.

"Yeah, that asshole, who I've been chasing for over a year. I'll be damned if I let Stefan Sanders get away when we're this close to catching him."

Levi was frustrated all right, on an epic roll that had a grin turning up the corners of Sean's mouth and a wider unguarded smile on Charlie's face. She thankfully wasn't taking Levi's vitriol personally. As for Sean, he'd no doubt zeroed in on how Levi's fire had also revived Marsh, both of them sitting taller—and closer. Marsh expected a conversation with him later like the ones he'd been having with Brax the past month. Hopefully, Sean would take a cue from Charlie and not take being left out of the loop until now personally.

"How did ASAC Byrne get assigned?" Levi asked.

"He's practically a Talley," Brax said. "And that whole crew is tight with the assistant director."

"They made moves before DC could stop them," Charlie said.

"DC could override them," Marsh countered. "Send in someone else."

"They could, but right now, they just want to sweep this under the rug."

"And pin it on Kwan."

"We're not going to let that happen," Holt said. "There's zero evidence she sent those chess boxes to Bell or Agent Kim." He spun his laptop on his knees, angled so he and Levi and Sean and Charlie could see the screen. It was video footage of a collection of bright white condos with blue roofs clustered around a courtyard.

"That's Kwan's complex in Encinitas," Levi said.

Holt zoomed in the footage as Kwan appeared through the locked gateway. "That's her entering on Thursday night."

"Time stamp matches," Marsh said. "That would be after Bell suspended us all."

Holt fast forwarded the footage. Kwan didn't leave her apartment again until a pair of uniforms escorted her out at six the next morning. "I collected footage from surrounding traffic and security cams. Plenty in that area." Holt zoomed back out, a satellite shot with numerous camera icons appearing on-screen. "There's no footage of Kwan leaving her condo. She was home all night. And there's no evidence on the web or in her financials that indicates she sent those boxes to anyone."

"Who took the chess box from her office?" Levi asked.

Holt's face fell. "Tapes are wiped."

And then so did Levi's, the rest of him slumping back against the hearth. He scrubbed his hands over his face, and Marsh waited for the silent scream to pass before gently drawing his hands down. He kept hold of one, a gesture Sean noticed, his smile growing wider. Marsh ignored his best friend and focused on his protégé instead. "There's a San Diego cyber agent, Farmer, if we need someone inside. He's good. We can trust him."

"Good," Holt said. "Helena's got Jax, our best hacker, with her, but there's only so much they can do without raising flags."

"I'll put them in touch if they aren't already."

"Can we track the box that was delivered to Matt?" Levi asked.

"Already on it," Holt confirmed.

"What else can we do?"

"You two"—Charlie waggled a finger at him and Levi—"can stay under the radar and let us work. You're both officially suspended."

"Passports?" Marsh asked.

"Still active," Brax answered. "Everyone's but Kwan's."

Levi's hand tensed in his. "You're going back to Europe?"

"Stefan Sanders is our best lead," Marsh replied, then shifted his gaze to Holt. "Has he left the country yet?" It was only a matter of time.

"Nothing official, but Eder is in the business of smuggling people. He's not the average person on the run."

"Can Mel—" Marsh started, only to be cut off by Levi who segued a different direction, squeezing his hand to draw his attention. "How far are we from Amarillo?"

"About six hours by car."

"Let's check there first," Levi said. "Assuming the Orchard building there was a front for Eder"—since Orchard was the West Coast front for Eder's trafficking operations—"Stefan could still be in the area."

"Do you really believe that?"

"No, I think he hightailed it out of there as soon as he got word we fucked his op, but he would've been in a hurry. I'm hoping he left some clues behind. Maybe some contacts or witnesses that can tell us more."

"All right, you do that." Here in Texas, close to David, who needed him more than Marsh did right now. Marsh could not take Levi away from his son after yesterday's near miss. "I'll get a jump on Europe."

"I'll have his back," Sean said.

Which earned him a shoulder punch from Charlie and a glare from Levi the likes of which Marsh had last seen across a restaurant table three weeks ago.

He turned his glare on Marsh and wrenched from his hold, standing. "Can I talk to you?" He didn't give Marsh a chance to object, disappearing around the hearth into the kitchen.

Marsh stood and aimed his own glare at Sean. "Not helping."

He shrugged and sank into the cushions. "You were being an idiot. Figured that would trigger the convo you two clearly need to have."

Marsh ignored his traitorous best friend and chased after his husband. He found him standing by the back door, hands on his hips, staring out at the pastures where Irina was checking on one of the pregnant goats. Levi's voice was low, carefully neutral when he spoke. "I thought we were on the same page after last night."

"We are." Marsh approached but didn't touch, sensing the spark waiting to ignite below Levi's controlled exterior. "I just don't want to lose these assholes."

Match lit, Levi spun and closed the distance between them, jabbing a finger at Marsh's chest. "I am not letting you run off after them alone."

"I won't be." Sean would have his back. Not as well as Levi would, no disrespect to his best friend, but this was the safest way to work both fronts at once.

"Without me," Levi seethed. "We're partners, and right now, David needs me here for at least a couple more days."

"You will be."

"He needs you too." He shoved Marsh's chest and paced the opposite direction, fuming.

A throat cleared behind them. Marsh turned to find Sean and Brax next to the hearth.

"I'll drop Trevor and Charlie back in DC, then go ahead to Europe," Sean said. "Start working our contacts there. I'll draw less attention, and I can poke around unofficially. Charlie will keep an ear out in DC and work anything we need there."

"And I can take you and Levi to Amarillo on the jet," Brax said. "Quick hop."

Neither of his best friends gave him room to argue, in their proposals or their stern expressions. Levi sealed the deal. "That'll work. Thank you."

"Put Jax on standby," Marsh told Brax. "I'll text Farmer. Have him assemble the team there for a call and prep him for assistance."

They both nodded, then faded back into the other room, leaving Marsh to face the wrath of a still simmering Levi. "I'm not trying to box you out," he said, lightly grasping Levi's arm, needing to reconnect and trying to forestall an explosion. "I know this is a lot." He gestured at the room of reinforcements behind them. "I'm just trying to move everyone on our side of the board into place while keeping you and David out of the center. He needs you safe. I need you safe."

Levi covered his hand and stepped closer, voice losing its angry edge, turning earnest in a way Marsh was powerless to resist. "I appreciate that, and I'm glad you have all these people at your back, but I'm at your side, Marsh. I'm your partner."

Marsh tapped his temple. "It's been a while here." Took Levi's hand in his and laid it over his heart. "Even longer here." Levi had spent the better part of yesterday afternoon and evening trying to repair cracks that Marsh kept chipping open. Doubt and fear were powerful jackhammers. "I might make some missteps."

"We'll make adjustments."

He drew Levi into his arms. "I just want to keep you and David safe."

Levi returned the embrace, hand flattening against his chest, words penetrating deep inside it. "Someone has to keep you safe too."

TEN

IT WAS late afternoon by the time Agent Farmer texted that he'd assembled the team in San Diego. When the video connected, Levi wasn't sure it was the right call, the drab walls and beeping sound unfamiliar. Not their war room at the FBI. But then Farmer's long, narrow face entered the frame. "Agent Bishop, good to see you." He nodded at Marsh beside him. "You too, Agent Marshall."

"Any issues connecting through the secure server?" Marsh asked.

"None. Thanks for saving me that trouble."

"You're not at the office," Levi said, still trying to get a bead on his location.

The cyber agent cut his dark eyes to the side. "Because someone demanded he also be on this call."

Farmer rotated his laptop, and in doing so, Levi got a better idea of their surroundings. IV stands, vitals monitors, shitty lighting. Those drab walls and beeping sounds made sense now. It didn't take a badge to guess who their guest of honor was.

Sure enough, Agent Kim appeared on-screen, elevated in a hospital bed, his head wrapped in bandages, a mop of black hair poking out the top. "These damn doctors won't discharge me yet," Matt griped, alert and irate.

"Your head got pin-balled, Matty K," said the dark-haired, dark-eyed Agent Byrne to Matt's right. His Boston brogue was thick, and if that didn't give away where he was from, the Red Sox T-shirt did. "It's still in a bandage, bro." He flicked a piece of errant gauze above Matt's ear, and Matt batted away his hand, grumbling.

"Matty K?" Marsh said with a smirk.

"Don't you start too." Matt jutted a thumb at Byrne. "Only he gets to do that."

"Agents Bishop and Marshall," the ASAC greeted. "It's good to see you again for longer than five seconds this time. Seems we have some friends in common besides this fucking Yankees fan."

Marsh knocked his knee under the table and leaned closer. "Don't tell him who you root for."

"If you two are done," said a familiar voice, and the laptop shifted again, widening the view, Alyssa and Will appearing in the frame. "Boss," Alyssa greeted followed by Will's, "Good to see you two alive and well."

As soon as the words were out, Will flicked his guilty gaze to Matt, and guilt likewise crawled up the back of Levi's neck. "Matt, I'm—"

"Nope, don't say it," Matt interrupted. "I said I was in."

Levi ran a hand over the back of his neck as if he could brush away the persistent, hypocritical feelings. He chuckled. "I've been telling Marsh the same thing the past thirty-six hours."

"Fuck," Matt cursed. "Is that all it's been?"

"How are you?" Levi asked. "Really?"

He pouted hilariously. "They took the good drugs away."

"Thank fuck for all our ears' sake," Byrne said.

"That's fair," Matt conceded. "Little bro got all the musical talent in the family."

"Gail?" Marsh asked.

If not for the harsh lighting, Levi might have missed the other agent's blush. "She's good. Just some cuts and scrapes. She's working with Kwan's attorney." He shivered dramatically. "Never met a woman that hot and that scary."

"With the two of them teaming up," Marsh said, "Kwan will be out in no time."

Levi would continue to worry that front until all charges against Kwan were dropped, but Gail was the best he'd ever seen in action, and Helena had a long line of frightened admirers. He had to trust the attorneys to do their jobs.

"All right, then," Byrne said. "Let's make sure your boss has progress to come back to."

Levi was sure his expression matched the skeptical ones of his other teammates. Everyone's except Matt's. Byrne must have sensed the mood shift. He lifted his hands, palms out. "Call those friends if you need to, but I'm on your side." Then he clasped Matt's shoulder. "Matt vouches for you, that's all I need, and it's my job to figure out what the fuck your SAC was up to."

SAC, not ASAC. The fact he was focused on Bell and not Kwan was a good sign. But why was it his focus at all? "I thought that was OPR's job," Levi said.

"They'll conduct their investigation, and I'll conduct mine. On behalf of my boss."

"The assistant director."

Byrne nodded. "I've got some experience with traitors in the ranks. That betrayal needs to be exposed and any of his allies gone before your ASAC takes over."

"You think she will?" Marsh asked.

"By all accounts, she was on track to succeed Bell or get an SAC post of her own. We'll do what we can to make sure she stays on that track. And personally, I want to see the work your team does continue. It's important, and the very last thing we need with trafficking and missing persons cases are dirty feds and dirtier politicians in the way of reuniting people or bringing families closure."

Byrne made a convincing pitch; Matt sealed it. "He vouches for me, Levi, and I vouch for him."

Given the current playing field, they could use all the help they could get, even a BoSox fan. Levi glanced at Marsh, who also gave a nod of approval. "Okay," Levi said, "let us catch you up."

He and Marsh took turns filling the group in on what they'd learned so far, then they started talking next steps. "We're headed to Amarillo tomorrow," Levi said. "We'll poke around the Orchard property and see if anyone has seen Stefan lately."

"We got any juice in that field office?" Marsh asked Byrne.

"I'll check."

"Appreciate it," Marsh said. "In the meantime, we need you"—he eyed the other agents—"looking into two angles."

"The missing chess set from Kwan's office," Matt said.

"And the missing footage," Farmer added.

"That's the first," Levi confirmed.

"Helena has a hacker with the Madigan team there in San Diego," Marsh relayed. "Name's Jax. I'll send you their contact info. If you need help, you can trust them."

"I brought one too," Byrne said, amusement dancing in his dark eyes.

"She might run away due to the coffee," Alyssa said, sounding more annoyed than amused. "She takes more sweetener than you," she said to Marsh.

"And she keeps muttering about earmuffs," Will added, landing somewhere closer to bemused. "It's ninety outside. I don't get it."

"She does that," Byrne said with a smile and a flit of his hand.

"The other angle, boss?" Alyssa asked, getting them back on track.

"Greg and Amanda Hudson," Levi said.

Matt gestured between him and Byrne. "That's where we've got the experience."

"Are we hopeful?" Byrne asked.

Grim faces all around, so Marsh spoke what they were all thinking. "Only if they were smart enough to run and hide before shit hit the fan."

"If Eder was willing to kill an SAC..." Alyssa said.

"And try to kill three agents and an attorney..." Will added.

"It doesn't look good," Levi finished. "But it's a lead we can't ignore." Speaking of open leads. "Did we get anything else out of the women we rescued?"

Alyssa shook her head. "Same story Dana gave us."

"Circle back with them in a couple days," Levi suggested. "Let the trauma wane, let them get resettled, then maybe more details will come to mind."

"I'll follow up with JoJo too," Matt said. "I'd bet Amanda approached more folks at the shelter."

"What do we do about Frederick?" Farmer asked.

"Keep him in protective custody," Marsh replied. "He's the last live link we have."

"Scratching his name on the top of my priority list," Byrne said. "Let us know what you find out in Amarillo."

"Will do," Levi said. "And thank you, Agent Byrne, for stepping in and making sure Matt doesn't try to do too much."

"Traitor!" Matt howled.

"It's Cam," Byrne said with a sneaky wink. "And you bet."

ELEVEN

THREE SHOUTS OF "CLEAR" and Levi returned from the open-concept bullpen to the reception area, flicking off his flashlight. There was no power in the cavernous industrial building, but this front area, with its large plate-glass windows, was bright enough from the morning sun outside. "I don't think Stefan was ever here."

"I don't think *anyone* has been here for weeks," Brax said as he cleared the bottom step from the lofted second floor. "None of the dust has been disturbed. No evidence that doors were opened or locks were turned."

"I noticed that too," Marsh said as he emerged from the shipping and receiving area at the back of the building. "The paint on the back door is peeling and the lock is rusty. If it had been opened, we'd expect to see chips, definitely a scrape in the dust." He turned to Levi. "Any evidence the appliances in the kitchen were used?"

Levi shook his head. "All of them were unplugged and turn-over clean. Fridge smelled like cleaner. No cool air and no food scents."

If they were keeping trafficking victims here, there would have at least been basics, not bare shelves and sparkly clean appliances. Same as the offices he'd passed in the hallway. "No equipment, cords, or other evidence of use in the offices either."

"I'm going to have a look around outside," Brax said. "See if there are any tracks or any cameras you or Holt can hack."

He moved to go, but the crunch of gravel outside sent them scrambling. Guns drawn, Brax stood behind the post of the open loft stairwell, Marsh crouched at the corner of the reception desk, and Levi hid in the shadow of the open door.

Closest to the stranger who's long thin shadow darkened the threshold.

Levi's gaze shot to Marsh's. Held. Fear was there but so too was confidence. On both their parts. Marsh gave a nod, and as the shadow extended an arm toward the door, Levi readied his weapon.

The stranger knocked. "FBI! Is someone in there?"

Levi breathed somewhat easier. "Friendlies," he answered as he lowered his weapon and stepped out from behind the door. He stood so Marsh and Brax still had clear lines of sight, just in case. "I'm putting away my gun and getting my badge." He moved slowly, as trained, and because the glare of the sun was denying him a good look at the new player. He flashed his badge. "I'm Special Agent Levi Bishop."

"Ah, that's a relief." The shadow stepped forward, out of the glare and into the daylight of the room. He was tall and wiry, white, with black-rimmed glasses that sat on a long thin nose, a matchstick vibe about him, amplified by the hipster attire—thin tie, tight vest, starched shirt, and a slim-fit suit. A bit overdressed for a Sunday in this heat, but the green eyes behind those glasses were bright and kind. "Special Agent Todd Barnes. I'm based out of Dallas." He waved in another agent. "This is Agent West, our local head in Amarillo." Agent West was shorter and stockier than Barnes, practically busting at the seams of his suit. The Black man's brown eyes were sharp and alert, tracking Marsh's and Brax's movements behind Levi.

Levi gestured their direction. "I'm with Special Agent Emmitt Marshall and Braxton Kane, a bail enforcement agent."

Tension receded, badges were flashed, and handshakes exchanged. "I thought we were meeting you at the field office," Marsh said.

"Got a tip from a mutual friend in San Francisco," Barnes said. "Seeing as you two are both suspended"—he waggled a finger at Levi and Marsh—"I thought not in the office would be better."

"He's a perpetual worrier," West said. "And my auntie owns the café across the street." He pointed at the Biscuit Kitchen storefront. "Knows we have this site locked down. She stopped by to pick up biscuits for church. Saw someone snooping around, so we booked it over here."

Church, Sunday in Texas, that explained the suits. Levi would've face-palmed if it wouldn't make him look ridiculous. "We should have called first, but it was on our way from the airport."

"And you wanted to nose around without locals looking over your shoulders," West said.

"I like you," Marsh drawled in his full Texas accent.

"Like you both actually. Would like you even better if you have some information for us."

Levi was on the same wavelength but tried a more diplomatic approach. "What my husband is trying to say is that we apologize for encroaching, though from our snoop around, it doesn't look like anyone has been here for a while."

Barnes waved off the apology. "Saved us all some hassle, and we can still get to church on time." He bumped the other agent's shoulder and a smile teased the corners of Agent West's lips.

"And you'd be right about this place," West said. "It's been quiet."

Barnes gestured them closer to the window and pulled a stack of rainbow-colored folders from under his arm. "Agent West and I spent the past twelve hours pulling together everything we can about this building." He handed Levi a green folder. "Transaction records. The deed is public record, but the other docs are from the escrow company. Pulled some strings."

Levi flipped through them, recognized the common denominator, and debated whether to gasp or curse. He settled on the latter—"Fuck"—and handed the folder to Marsh. "All the Orchard docs are signed by Catherine Sanders."

"Surprise, surprise."

"Was she ever here?" Brax asked the other agents.

West shook his head. "Building was bought sight unseen."

"Through an agent?"

"Commercial broker, Brooks Patton." Barnes handed over a yellow file. "Overgrown frat-boy type. Talked to him this morning. He thought he was buying a building for some British company."

West rolled his eyes. "Told damn near everyone about it, including my auntie."

"For real?" Marsh said.

"He's not the sharpest tool in the shed. He's the perfect broker if you don't want someone to look too closely. Took his five percent and happily shuffled paper."

"But someone did check out the site," Barnes said. "About four months ago before the prior tenants moved out. They had saved security footage." He handed Levi the red folder.

He flipped it open and froze, recognizing the visitor's cropped hair, bulky build, and neck and forearm tattoos. Not the first security stills he'd seen of the man. "Stefan Sanders."

Marsh slid one hand into the groove of Levi's back and with the other tugged the folder from his white-knuckle grip.

Barnes seemed to sense the danger, his chipper voice taking on a worried tone that better aligned with the perpetual worrier West had described. "He said he repre-sented a developer who was looking to invest in the area. Asked if they were interested in selling. They told him they were tenants with a couple months left on their lease and gave him the landlord's contact info."

"Did the landlord ever hear from Stefan?" Marsh asked.

"No," West answered. "All contact was through Brooks."

"Not sure whether this last bit of info is good or bad for you." Barnes held out a blue folder. "Stefan Sanders was here on Thursday."

Another photo still. Of a place Levi had just walked through. "The airport."

"He was using an alias. Damon Wyatt."

Levi flipped the page and scanned the boarding pass and fake passport. This wasn't an alias on their list. New? Using an ID created by Blake Anthony?

"We made an educated guess as to his destination and sure enough, one of the gate agents recognized him."

"Houston?" Marsh said, then explained to Levi, "It's the closest airport with the most outbound international flights."

West nodded. "Houston, then on to Munich."

Which meant he'd gotten word of their bust, that the transport would not arrive, and had promptly left. Which meant he hadn't been in San Diego to deliver those boxes. Which meant by now he was probably back in Vienna.

Barnes read their cringes correctly. "Bad news, then?"

"Bit of both," Levi said, then focused on the good news part. "Means there's not likely to be another transport here."

"But it also means he's out of our jurisdiction," Marsh said, and by the determined set of his husband's jaw, Levi knew they'd be having that conversation about going to Europe sooner rather than later.

TWELVE

THE DRIVE back to the airport was a short one spent mostly in silence, Levi ignoring any effort Marsh made to engage him. He just kept flipping through the colorful folders Agent Barnes had given him, muttering curses under his breath. The news wasn't all bad, but Marsh had to concede more of it was bad than good.

Their prime suspect had slipped through their fingers again. A man Levi had been tracking almost as long as Marsh. Was that why he'd closed off on the car ride over? Why he'd left Marsh and Brax standing in the plane's galley, stomped down the aisle, and plopped into the back row window seat? Had the altitude sickness gotten to him again? Or was it because Levi was as equally unenthused as Marsh about the conversation ahead? Each time they'd tried to have it the past couple days, the train jumped the tracks. But Marsh had a different perspective now, a valuable reminder of the competent federal agent he was lucky to call his husband. A fact he couldn't let himself forget, no matter how strong his protective instincts.

"I'm going to ping Mel and Holt," Brax said as the copilot closed the plane door behind them. "Update them and get the latest to our contacts in Europe."

"There isn't an official bounty on Stefan yet." Marsh lifted a hand to count off all the ways this was outside the best friend scope. "No charges have been filed, no bail set and broken, and from what Charlie said, there likely won't be. I can't ask—"

"You didn't."

"Brax."

"This is what we do. Redemption Inc. and the Madigans. Not every bounty is on the books, especially when it's the kind of evil we want to stop."

Marsh squinted his eyes like he wasn't sure who he was seeing. "Did you really used to be a cop?"

"I made my peace with where I can do the most good, including for my family, which you are a part of too," he said with a crooked smile while still managing to sound grumpy about it. Yep, same ole Brax, same good to the core center under layers of grizzle. "Deal with us."

"I think that's more the other way around these days."

"It shakes out in the end. I'll call Sean too." He patted Marsh's shoulder and jutted his chin toward the back of the plane. "Go check on your husband."

Time to have that conversation, regardless of whether Marsh or Levi wanted to. He grabbed two bottles of water from the galley, then made his way down the row and slid into the seat next to Levi.

Levi spoke before Marsh had the chance to. "Don't even start with that go-it-alone-to-Europe bullshit."

Maybe Levi wasn't so hesitant to have the conversation after all.

Marsh removed his hat and tossed it into the seat across the aisle. "I won't be alone."

"Correct." Levi shifted onto the hip nearest Marsh and leaned closer. "Because your partner will be with you."

"What about David?" Marsh kept speaking before Levi could protest. "I want you at my side. Make no mistake about that. You are the best partner, the best agent, I have worked with, but David has to come first. Stopping Stefan and Eder won't matter if David is compromised, physically or emotionally." He clasped Levi's hand and ran a thumb over his wedding band. "It's why you put this ring on your finger. You were trying to do what was best for him, to keep the roof over his head and be there for him more."

Levi didn't immediately object. He spun the ring around his finger and after several moments said, "You're right."

"So you'll stay?" A question, not a statement. It had to be Levi's choice for David.

But that wasn't where Levi's head had gone. "Is there a reason you don't want me in Europe?" Gaze downcast, he spun his ring again. "Sean or someone—"

Marsh leaned across the armrest, clasped Levi's chin, and kissed him hard, tongue parting Levi's lips and sweeping inside, claiming the only thing he wanted. He drew back when Levi started to lean in, to want more himself, more than they could claim together in their current surroundings. And not without resolving the disagreement at hand. "There's nothing for me in Europe but a job and a sad apartment. You are the only partner I want, personally and professionally. But I know what it's like to lose a parent. So does David. We were both lucky to have another parent who moved the world for us. But if I'd lost my moms too, I don't—" He rested his forehead against

Levi's shoulder and shook his head. "I can't be the one who takes you away from David. I'd never forgive myself. I still haven't forgiven myself for Friday." The go-it-alone-to-Europe plan had initially been about protecting Levi and to some extent himself, but when it came right down to it, the person who truly mattered was the one they were both responsible for, who couldn't protect himself from the evil encroaching on their world.

Levi's fingers threaded through his hair, and he kissed the crown of his head. "David's lucky to have someone else in his corner now too. So am I. We can't lose you either. I have commitments to both of you and to my job."

Marsh lifted his head and braced his forearms on the armrest, his fingers tangling with Levi's. "Per the Bureau, we're both suspended."

"The oath I took says I still have a job to do. You said we'd be safe at the ranch. Is there any reason to think David won't be if I go with you?"

"Of course not. No one knows that land better than my moms, and we can call in more reinforcements."

Levi squeezed his fingers. "Give me until tomorrow. Let's make sure we know where all the pieces are on the board and the plays we need to make."

Marsh couldn't help but smile. "Someone's been paying attention."

"Hard not to with all you chess nerds around." Levi rolled his eyes but turned serious the next second. "We'll get all the information and make an assessment. Then we'll talk to David, tell him as much as we can, and we'll let it be his call."

That was all Marsh could ask.

THIRTEEN

STORMS DELAYED their arrival back at the ranch. And wreaked havoc on an understaffed Mi Herencia. Once they did arrive, they'd immediately jumped into action. Marsh and Brax rode out with Camilla to help suppress a brush fire in the south pasture while Levi had driven the ATV alongside Irina and David on horseback to round up a flock of sheep that had escaped through a gap in the fence caused by a downed tree. Holt stayed at the house with Lily, monitoring and coordinating efforts in real time between the two groups and the local fire department. It had been after midnight by the time the fire was contained, the sheep tucked safely in a barn, and everyone safe and accounted for back at the house, chowing down on the pulled pork Holt had cooked up in the Crock-Pot for when they returned.

"It's not that late," Camilla had said, and she'd laughed out loud at the look Levi had shot her. "All in a summer day's work."

He and Marsh had had some late nights the past month

but nothing quite like that. Add the extra hour they'd stayed up after eating—reviewing the latest intel Holt had gathered and considering their options for next steps—and neither he nor Marsh had had any trouble sleeping through the night.

Unfortunately, crisis management had delayed their talk with David, and in the middle of downtown Alpine at the July Fourth parade wasn't the best place to have that chat either. And besides, David's slack-jaw wonder at every turn —the parade, the decked-out town, the livestock displays, the booths of games for kids and culinary goodies for everyone else—was worth putting off the convo a few more hours.

"Like, July Fourth is a big deal in San Diego, but this is wild," David said as he walked backward ahead of them, finishing his second helping of disgusting Frito pie.

"Small town Americana," Marsh said with a wry smile.

Levi could see the appeal—of some of it. The food; the good cheer; the sparkling clean, festive town; the community, which was more diverse than he would have expected. Less appealing were the open-carry guns and beer, but he tried to focus less on the unsavory aspects and more on the good parts that excited Lily and David.

Well, everything but the Frito pie. "If you ever bring that into my house," he said to Marsh, "I will divorce you."

The jab was out before Levi could catch it, the presumption too much, he worried, but neither Marsh nor David seemed to blink.

Marsh held him tighter to his side and rolled with it as if Levi hadn't just painted a picture of life after this case, back in San Diego, all of them together. "Noted," he said with a wide smile. Then held a fist out for David to bump. "We'll save it for when he's on assignment."

"Deal." David bumped back, then pitched his empty disgusting dip container into a trash bin before falling into step beside them. "You really grew up here?"

"You don't believe it?"

He shrugged. "No offense, but you just seem so loud, so much bigger than this."

"We never know what a person's background is," Levi said, adjusting for the assumption. While Marsh wouldn't think poorly of him for the statement, someone on the receiving end of a future assumption might.

"You're not wrong," Camilla chimed in. "High school teachers will tell you he was the loudest one in class."

"The smartest too," Irina added.

And the most well liked, judging by the number of people who had stopped to welcome Marsh home, to ask how life and work were treating him, to congratulate him when he introduced his new husband and stepson. Out of the many, only one had given them an askance look, the old vet Irina had once interned for before she'd left to work with Camilla on the ranch.

"Irina!" David bounced on his toes and pointed at the line of food tents ahead. "There's another kolaches stand. I wonder what filling they have." He was gone before Levi could tell him twenty kolaches was already too many.

"Do you know how to make those?" he asked Marsh. "I might also have to divorce you if the answer is no."

Marsh hugged him tighter. "Quit threatening to divorce me. A husband might get a complex." He dropped a kiss on his temple. "And yes, I know how to make them. Irina's grandmother was Czech. They're a holiday staple."

They meandered behind the rest of the family, Marsh's arm over his shoulder, Levi's slung around his waist, sampling this or that treat and cheering on David as he won stuffed toys for Lily. It was a happy day, one Levi couldn't have imagined after the last few. One like they hadn't had in years. Hell, one like they'd never really had before. "Thank you," he said to Marsh. "For giving him this experience."

"What experience?"

"This." He gestured at all the activity around them. "He was born and raised in San Diego, same as me, same as my parents. And Kristin and her family were from LA. I don't know if he ever would have had this if you hadn't come into our lives."

Levi liked the blush that pinked Marsh's bronze cheeks, the pleased easy smile that stretched across his face and had been hiding since Friday. Levi missed it more than he should. "I like it here." Liked that it was what Marsh, David, and the rest of their friends and family had needed after last week's roller coaster.

"Good," Marsh said. "But please don't tell me you want to move here because, as much as I love it too, David was right. I am loud. I need more."

"But it was good growing up here?"

Marsh glanced around fondly but not without some reservation. "It was what I needed. Space to roam, the land and culture that connected me to my roots, and the college does tend to make the area somewhat less conservative than other parts of west Texas."

"Folks seem accepting."

"Relatively, and by now, they're used to my moms. They don't take any shit, and I was always big enough to fend for myself. But it wasn't always easy, and as soon as I could, I pulled a Camilla and got the hell out of here."

He'd stayed gone—twenty-plus years in the service, then Europe with the FBI. But it sounded like Marsh was back more often recently, like he fit into the fold here no matter how long he was gone. "Has coming back gotten easier over the years?"

He nodded. "That sense of connection is still here. It was always a safe haven, a place where I'd come to lick my wounds." Wounds—some intentional, some not—that had left him feeling somehow unworthy when he was the furthest thing from it. Levi tangled their fingers together, gave Marsh the moment of reflection, past and present, he needed. "But it's been different the last couple years," Marsh said as they crossed Main Street on the way to another set of food tents, this time Holt charging ahead of everyone for what looked like homemade carrot cake. "I've been able to share this place with others more. I like that."

With a family, born and found, that hadn't let Marsh forget he was loved, a family Levi was happy he and David were welcomed into, one he wanted to be a part of longer. Because despite Marsh's protective streak, despite the walls that were thrown up and knocked down this weekend, seeing Marsh in his element with his friends and family, hearing Marsh put him and David first, had Levi falling even harder for his husband. "I'm glad you brought us here too."

"I repeat, do not get any ideas about moving here."

The altitude sickness was enough to nix that possibility. And even if it wasn't, there was an even more powerful force to reckon with, one that would find a way to keep them in California no matter what. "You think my mother would let us leave San Diego?"

Marsh laughed out loud, turning heads all around, but none the way he'd turned Levi's three weeks ago, like he continued to do every day.

FOURTEEN

AS THE SUN DESCENDED SLOWLY, questions flew fast and furious around the picnic table—this or that, true or false, have you ever—everyone playing along as they waited for the fireworks to start, the view from the ranch's higher ground the second-best seat in town, according to Marsh. Levi idly wondered what the best was while the current question—real caviar versus Texas caviar—made a loop around the table.

"Real," Marsh answered, and Levi made himself dizzy with how fast he jerked his gaze to him. His wasn't the only shocked expression at the table. "What?" Marsh cut a glance through all of them. "Y'all act like I ain't got a bit of finery."

David propped an elbow on the table, hand in the air, counting off with his fingers. "Y'all… Ain't… Finery…"

Marsh nailed him square in the face with his balled-up napkin, everyone laughing before picking the round robin inquiry back up. Dunkin or Krispy Kreme? Beach or mountains? *Great British Bake-Off* or *Hell's Kitchen*? They carried on like that, getting to know one another better, until Camilla and Holt started clearing plates. Lily was reaching the end of her rope, squirming and interrupting, rubbing her eyes with her fists, frowning more than smiling, on the cusp of a wail. Telltale signs any parent would pick up on, including her father. Brax stood, plucked Lily off Marsh's lap, and settled her on his hip. "Someone's up way past her bedtime."

"But firewoks," she protested, even as her head hit her father's shoulder.

Brax grinned and dropped a kiss on her auburn curls. "I'll show you firewoks when we get back to San Francisco." Clearly, hilariously not the same thing, but Lily was too tired to catch on, her eyelids drooping.

"I'll be right behind you," Holt said as he reached between Marsh and Levi to grab their plates. "Hold confirmations are in your inbox," he told them. "Finalize the booking when you're ready."

"Bookings for what?" David asked.

He and Marsh waited for everyone else to clear out, which was a dead giveaway to a kid as smart as David. "Y'all have been buttering me up all day, haven't you?"

Levi raised a brow. "Y'all?"

"His fault." David waggled a finger at Marsh. "And you didn't answer the question?"

"That wasn't buttering you up," Marsh said. "That was a whole day with family and without a crisis."

He held his hands up as if in worship. "Miracles do happen."

Levi balled up his own napkin and threw it at his snark-monster child.

David snatched it out of the air, laughing. "So we have

to go home? You have to go back to work?" He didn't seem overly nervous about going back to San Diego. A good sign. But that unfortunately wasn't the plan yet.

"We do have to go to work," Marsh said, "but not in San Diego."

David's snark and bravado vanished. "Both of you?" he said, voice cracking.

Levi reached across the table and gently clasped his son's wrist. "Marsh is my partner. I promised to have his back."

"But—" Marsh was no doubt going to give him an out, but David beat him to the most obvious question.

"Where?"

"Europe," Marsh said instead. "The Hague, where I lived and worked, then likely on to Vienna, where we think our suspect is headed."

"I thought the FBI didn't have authority overseas. How does that work?"

David's tone indicated the question was more argumentative than anything, a counter for why they shouldn't leave him, but there was also genuine curiosity underlying it. Levi took a few minutes to explain about legal attachés, cyber agents, and how, despite the FBI having no jurisdiction outside the US, the Bureau's presence abroad was critical for working with counterpart agencies, domestic and international, in an increasingly global world. Marsh then told him about his own work and how after 9/11, terrorism and transnational organized crime had collided and gone global. Levi had started to object several times—worried the level of detail wouldn't help David's anxiety—but Marsh's hand on his thigh beneath the table forestalled him.

"Sean used to do this?" David asked once they were done. "Before he left the FBI?"

Marsh nodded.

"Why can't he have your back? Why's it have to be my dad?"

Marsh deflated before Levi's eyes, every fear he'd voiced yesterday repeated.

"David," Levi tempered, only to have David jerk back.

"I'm not good with this anymore."

Marsh patted Levi's thigh. "It's fine. He's right."

He was a scared kid. That didn't make him right necessarily. Levi stood, circled the end of the table, and crouched next to the bench where David sat, angling him with a gentle hand on his shoulder. "If you don't want me to go, I won't, but let me explain why I want to."

He bit his lips, eyes glassy, but nodded. Willing to listen was far more than he would've gotten out of David a month ago. He'd grown so much, and he understood now why Marsh had given him details. Because he'd earned it and because it provided context for what Levi needed to explain.

"Your mom brought me this case. She was working to get a client asylum, and the woman disappeared. She was at-risk, an immigrant with an opportunistic family."

"Someone sold her?"

"Your mom thought so. I don't know if I'll ever find her —the chances are slim at this point—but even if I can't find her, there are other women and at-risk victims we can help. Help them like I couldn't help your mom." He swallowed hard around the knot in his throat. "I will always wonder if I could have done more."

This time David grasped his hand. "She died of cancer. You know you couldn't."

He looked his son square in the eyes and made him face a hard truth. "You don't wonder the same, even knowing that?"

David cast his gaze aside, not liking it, but nodded, conceding the point. Sometimes the heart overruled the brain, no matter how irrational.

"In this case," Levi said, "I can do more. You're right. I'm not a doctor. I didn't have the skill set to help your mom. Hell, a whole team of doctors couldn't. But in this instance, I do have the skill set, and I have a partner that makes me even better at what I do." He glanced across the table at Marsh, then back to David. "But we both agreed this is your call. You've already lost one parent. You say the word, and I stay here."

David's gaze strayed across the table. "He makes you better at your job too?"

"Your father is the best agent I've ever worked with."

"What about Sean?"

Marsh leaned forward and whispered, "He doesn't need to know."

David's chuckle was watery but a laugh nonetheless. God, what had they done to deserve Marsh in their lives? Someone who so effortlessly fit, who brought humor and warmth back to them when the chill had settled for so long. David released Levi's hand, wiped his eyes, and took a deep breath. "Okay, do I stay here? What can I do to help?"

Levi stood and drew his son into a hug, dropping a kiss on his head. "You are the bravest person I know."

Marsh reached across the table for David's hand. "We'd like you to stay here. We feel it's safest."

He nodded.

"Keep in touch," Levi said. "Every day, with us and back home. I might not always be able to monitor the situation there, so I'm depending on you to be my eyes and ears."

"Same goes for the ranch," Marsh said. "You'll be safe here, but stay alert. I'll show you the security setup in the morning if that'll make you feel better."

David's eyes brightened, another point in the trust column. "It would. Thank you." He glanced between the two of them once more. "Will you be safe there? At The Hague and in Vienna?"

"We'll be safer together." Levi clasped his shoulder, bent so they were eye level, and gave him the truth. "I will do everything in my power to come back to you."

Marsh went a step further. "And I'll make sure of it."

FIFTEEN

"SO THIS IS what that secret smirk was about the other night." Levi stood at the edge of the ranch's highest mesa, staring out over the hillside of sunflowers, the towering crop cast in a silvery glow from the moon's reflection off the stream that snaked through the valley floor. He turned, and his blue eyes were aglow too, giving Levi that wolfy quality that had first captured Marsh's imagination. Much like the view tonight had captured Levi's. "Those are Irina's sunflowers?"

"They're planted in a few different spots on the ranch, but this is the largest field. I wanted to show you during the daylight, but those hours kept slipping away from us." Marsh lowered the tailgate of the utility vehicle they'd driven out in and hopped up on it. "I also told you I'd show you my favorite place on the property." He held his arms open wide, gesturing to the field of yellow flowers, the glistening stream, the plentiful pastures on the other side that stretched all the way to the house, where a glowing fire pit cast enough light to see four adults sitting around it. But

Marsh's mind was still on the teenager they'd left inside the house, on the maturity David had shown earlier that night, on the risk they were asking him to take after losing so much already. "Do you think David will be okay? The last thing I want to do is hurt him more. Not for me."

Levi hopped onto the tailgate beside him. "Did you consider going to Hanover U?"

Marsh startled at the non sequitur. Levi had a habit of those, but they usually led to a point, so Marsh followed along. "Applied. Didn't tell my father. Didn't matter since I didn't get in."

"Explain something to me." He shifted, bending a knee up onto the tailgate and angling toward Marsh. "How do you not understand your worth?" He tilted his head toward the house. "Those two women down there know it. Your best friends know it. How can I make you understand it?" He laid a hand on Marsh's chest. "In here."

The heat from Levi's hand seeped through his shirt, and Marsh folded both hands over his, trapping that warmth where he wanted it most. He held Levi close and confessed a truth he'd never told anyone. "They all left." His voice cracked, a deeper version of David's earlier. He cleared his throat and started again. "Jefferson. Patrick. Brax. Sean. I can't blame the latter two, but it still hurt. Like I wasn't enough."

Levi tugged at his hand, and Marsh loosened his grip, then tensed when Levi made to move farther away. Had he said too much, leaned too much on a man who'd already given him more than he could ask for? But then Levi rose onto his knees and threw one over Marsh's lap, straddling him. He forced his gaze up into those eerily gorgeous blue eyes, the moonlight and conviction making them burn.

"I'll talk to David again in the morning before we leave and make sure he's still good. And if he's not, I'll stay." He framed Marsh's face in his hands. "But even if I'm here, and you're there, I will not leave you. I want to know every move you make. My case was yours. Your case is mine."

Marsh tried for a joke, anything to stop his heart from beating out of his chest, from exploding with hope. "Community property?"

"Something like that. And something like this." Levi laid a kiss on him similar to the one the other night, plundering and claiming, but slower and more deliberate, befitting the quiet night, the heaviness of the decisions they'd made, and the discussions they'd had today. Full of the promises floating in the summer air around them. Levi drew back and rested their foreheads together, his breath ghosting over Marsh's lips with words he'd waited a lifetime to hear. "I will have your back, however I can do that, however you need me to, and I will give you a home and heart to return to. I promise I won't leave you."

Marsh struggled to accept Levi's words were meant for him. "I want to believe you."

"Have I given you any reason not to?"

He hadn't. Levi had surprised him, stood by him, comforted him, and trusted him. Marsh wanted to believe, more than anything, that Levi meant every word of his promise. That the man kissing a path down his throat felt the respect, admiration, and affection Marsh had for him. That the hands sneaking under his shirt and racing up his back meant to claim and hold him like Marsh wanted him to, for as long as Levi would have him.

Levi kissed the hinge of his jaw. "I took a chance on you

that night in the restaurant." The corner of his lips. "Take a chance on me now."

Marsh owed him that much—a chance and his trust. Same as Levi had given him when they hadn't known each other at all. Same as Levi had trusted his family with him. Marsh and his heart felt safe with the man in his arms. This wouldn't end like all the times before. Levi's words, his kiss, promised more. Marsh decided to take a chance. "I'm trusting you."

"I won't let you down," Levi mumbled against his lips. "Should we move this back to the house, then?"

Marsh drew back and brushed the long top strands off Levi's forehead. "Aww, my sweet city boy. If you think this is the first time someone has fucked on this ride, I have two horny women to introduce you to."

Levi threw his head back and laughed, the sound unlocking all the hope Marsh had trapped inside himself, the sight every inch the sexy wolf that turned Marsh on like no one else ever had. He leaned forward and flicked his tongue in the divot exposed by Levi's V-neck tee. Levi gasped, thrust, and clasped the back of his head, holding him there. "Yeah, baby, just like that."

Fingers tunneled through his hair, and Marsh groaned, kissing and licking every inch of skin he could reach, rocking his hips as Levi's other hand dug into his shoulder blade beneath his shirt.

Marsh reached between Levi's legs and palmed his cock. Levi tried to stifle his groan, and Marsh shook loose of his hold, tilting back his head to meet Levi's gaze. "I don't think they can hear you scream from here. But I can, and I want to hear it. Maybe that'll convince me."

Fire blazed in Levi's eyes. "Is that a challenge?"

"Is that what you want? A challenge?" At Levi's nod, Marsh surged up, flipped them so Levi was stretched beneath him on the utility vehicle's bed. "Get our dicks out and make us come. I want you to scream for me, Levi."

Levi arched, hips rocking up, like he couldn't stop the need for friction, but the next second, he went to work, unfastening buckles and zippers, fingers slipping whenever Marsh would suck his neck or bite his nipples through his shirt. Growling, Levi wrapped a leg over his hip and squeezed. "Stop that," he demanded. "If you don't, I'm going to come in my pants like a teenager, and I would at least like to get to the frottage portion of fucking in the back of a truck."

Marsh pushed up on his forearms and smirked. "Fantasy of yours, Bishop?"

"No." Levi's tone shifted, soft and earnest, his eyes going liquid to match. "This is my reality now, and I'd like to scream for my husband."

Marsh groaned, his hips pumping down, Levi's words twin arrows to his heart and his dick. Which he needed Levi's hand on. Now. "I'll behave. I promise."

Levi uncurled his leg, giving Marsh room to maneuver again, and within seconds, their pants and boxers were around their thighs, their cocks bumping. Levi made a show of licking his palm, made Marsh's cock drip, then reached down to grasp them together.

And stroked.

Marsh's arms and legs shook, his breath shook, his world shook.

"We need to switch?" Levi asked.

"No, you just keep doing that, and we'll both be screaming in no time."

Levi smiled wolfishly, and picked up the pace, fast and rough, neither of them about slow and gentle this time.

Marsh stretched over him, forearms on either side of his head, framing his whole world. Their corner of it tonight filled with frantic thrusts and claiming kisses, sweat-soaked shirts and straining muscles, groans that built, pleasure that mounted, until their screams broke loose, the two of them falling apart together.

SIXTEEN

MARSH STOOD under an umbrella in front of the American embassy at The Hague, his husband giving the monolithic structure a head-tilted assessment. "It's more brick than I thought it would be."

"The building or The Hague in general?"

"Both," Levi answered. "But the brick buildings we passed on the way here were at least dressed up. Baroque-like but brick. This is just…" He struggled to find the word, finally landing on "Boxy. Like a Volvo in building form."

Marsh laughed almost as loud as the clap of thunder that heralded heavier rain on the way. "As long as it does the job of protecting the people inside like a Volvo does, then it can be boxy."

"Fair."

"You'll get your baroque embassy in Vienna." He handed the umbrella to Levi and dug his badge out of his pocket. "Enjoy the comforts of a modern embassy building while you can."

"Now I'm worried."

Marsh smirked, "You should be. Come on. Let's get inside before this shower turns into a downpour."

Inside, though, only extended to the embassy's soaring glass lobby. Big Sal, as everyone in the building called the hulking Marine who manned the employee entrance, ushered them through the metal detectors but stopped them from going further. "I'm obligated to let you in with these." Big Sal handed back his and Levi's passports, then handed Marsh his hat.

"And because I saved your ass that one time in the desert." Marsh had known Big Sal longer than either of their tenures at The Hague. Had known him since he was an eighteen-year-old jarhead who'd followed a girl to a remote village and gotten stuck in enemy territory with only Marsh to guide him out.

"And I will buy you a beer anytime for that save, but I got orders, Colonel."

"From who?"

"Me." Special Agent Binu Patel strode across the lobby, two staffers carrying file boxes on his heels.

Binu had been Sophie's boss before he'd moved over to Europol and she'd moved into the head legat post. He'd moved back after Sophie's death, in a temporary capacity that had lasted more than three years now. He was a damn fine lawyer, a good agent, and a decent boss, if a bit stuffy in his tailored three-piece suits and shiny shoes. He generally left Marsh alone to run his cyber cases as he saw fit as long as they got closed. It had only been him and Binny since Sean had left, plus the couple of rotating staffers. He didn't have time to micromanage.

Binu ground to a halt in front of Marsh and Levi.

"You're suspended," he said to Marsh, then to Levi, "And so are you, Agent Bishop."

So much for polite introductions. "Levi, my boss, Special Agent Binu Patel."

Levi cocked a brow. "You have a boss?"

Fair question. Marsh hadn't exactly been reporting in regularly, but he had been working. "I wasn't tracing counterfeits in Hong Kong for shits and giggles."

Binu sighed. "The shits and giggles you left me to deal with."

"I left it practically solved. You just had to coordinate an arrest with our counterparts in Hong Kong."

"You left me a mountain of paperwork for that case, your case, your transfer, and now a suspension. As if I wasn't already understaffed."

Marsh could see where maybe this was a situation Binu was obliged to manage. "Look, Binny, I can explain."

"No, you can take your things and go." He pointed at the ground in front of his and Levi's feet and the staffers dropped the boxes there.

Heavy ones, judging by the thud they made.

Curious, as the sum total of Marsh's things still in his office that mattered would fit in a shoe box, and they certainly weren't thud heavy.

He glanced back up at Binu, seeing the imperfections he'd missed on first glance. Hair styled in its usual pompadour but overlong with strands of silver peeking through the black. Skin more wheatish than the rich tanned brown it typically was in summer. Suit on-point but hanging loose, looking store-bought, which would normally scandalize Binny. More cheekbone and darker under eyes than Marsh was used to seeing on the perpetually overworked legat. But despite the signs of exhaustion Marsh detected on second look, Binu's coal black eyes burned with intensity, with anger that, if Marsh was correct, wasn't directed at them.

It was a wonder he didn't breathe fire when he spoke again. "At this rate, I'm going to have to recruit Ajay to help staff this place when he's back in town tomorrow."

Ajay Patel was Binu's brother and a retired CIA agent who ran a gastropub on the coast a block over from Marsh's building. It had been the unofficial meeting place for their team whenever they'd needed to discuss sensitive matters out of earshot of embassy eavesdroppers. It was where he and Binny had discussed Marsh's plan to potentially intercept Eder Capital through what appeared to be related crimes in San Diego.

Appearances *then* had been correct, and so was Marsh *now* about the direction of Binny's anger. Bending, Marsh stacked the boxes, then hefted them together. "You're in charge of the umbrella," he said to Levi. "Don't want anything in here to get wet."

Binu aimed a tight smile Levi's direction. "I'm sorry we couldn't meet under better circumstances, Agent Bishop." Without another word, he turned and strode back across the lobby, disappearing around the wall to the elevator bank.

"Don't say a word," Marsh mumbled to Levi before saying goodbye to Big Sal on their way out the door. Near the curb, he braced a foot on the retaining wall and balanced the boxes on his knee. As much as he wanted to open them, he didn't dare in the rain or in range of the embassy's cameras. He jutted his opposite hip at Levi. "Use my phone to call the car."

"What just happened?" Levi asked as they waited for the call to connect.

"Sean's been working our contacts. We have a meeting with Binny and his ex-spy brother tomorrow." He patted the side of the boxes. "To discuss whatever's in these."

SEVENTEEN

LEVI DISAGREED with Marsh that his Netherlands apartment was sad. The balcony view of the North Sea kept it from being that. But what lay behind Levi inside the apartment was the definition of generic. A square box on the second floor of a square brick building. He really didn't think The Hague would be so brick. Marsh's one-bedroom rental had a basic kitchen with a dining bar and a rectangular table, the latter already covered in papers, a living area with a futon and chair, a bedroom and bathroom on the other side of the wall. Prefurnished if Levi had to guess, and together with the bland white walls, zero personality. Not an ounce of the character possessed by the man who inhabited the space.

But did Marsh really live here? Levi didn't think so. He'd been right that evening on the patio back in San Diego; this place wasn't home to Marsh. It was a place to work that wasn't the office and a place to occasionally sleep. Levi hated that Marsh had lived like this. Someone with so much color in his heart and soul had no business being stuffed inside a sterile box. It made Levi's offer of a home seem less like an overstep and more like the escape Marsh had needed. Made the equation between them more balanced than Levi had realized. He'd given Marsh something he'd truly needed. Not enough, not compared to what Marsh had given him and David but more significant than Levi had initially thought.

The balcony door opened behind him. "You want to come in from the rain? I made you some leaf water."

Levi stretched out an arm, flitting his hand in the light drizzle. "The change of weather is nice."

"We're not moving here either."

Levi ducked his chin and hid his secret smile, the one that appeared every time Marsh implied they were going to continue living together. In San Diego, Levi hoped. And hope was what he aimed to instill in Marsh. The doubts and pessimism lingered from all the times Marsh had not been chosen, but Levi was starting to win him over, starting to make him believe. Small victories. He pushed off the balcony rail and followed Marsh inside.

"You send David a picture?" Marsh asked.

Levi held up his phone, his text thread with David displayed, a picture of the North Sea filling the screen. "For your mothers' sake, I hope it didn't wake him. Five-in-the-morning David is a beast." He pocketed his phone and grabbed his tea off the bar, reflexively lifting it to inhale. Peppermint tickled his senses, his favorite, the first he'd had in days. It was a wonderful, considerate surprise that helped settle him after days of travel. "Thank you."

"You're welcome." He waited for Levi to join him at one end of the table, then pointed at the box on the opposite end. "That one is full of case files. The bombing that killed Sophie, Eder Capital, their role in wider trafficking operations, everything our TOC task force was working on."

"Don't you have all that electronically?"

"I do. If I know Binny, this is his version of doc retention."

"By moving the files out of the building?"

Marsh nodded. "DC must have gotten to him."

"Not before Charlie and I did." Sean emerged from the bedroom, mug in hand. He made a beeline for the kitchen and the fresh pot of coffee Marsh had brewed. "Glad you got in."

"Thanks for the lift," Levi said, referring to the private car Sean had sent to the airport for them.

"Would've been there myself, but I had a call with our London office. I'm relatively on their time zone for a change, and they are taking full advantage." He rounded the dining bar and stood on the other side of the table. "So if those are our files, what was in the other box?"

Marsh spread his hands, indicating the files and papers covering the table. "Binny's investigation."

"Binny's?" Levi would have thought the acting legat's files would have been included with the others from the office.

"Into Sophie's murder."

Sean didn't seem surprised. "He wouldn't admit to it when I caught him outside the tea shop yesterday, but I gathered he was running something separate."

"He looks rough," Marsh said.

Sean wore a concerned expression to match. "Noticed that too."

"Who was she to him?" Levi asked. "More than a colleague?"

"She was his friend and protégé."

"Pretty sure he also carried a torch for her," Marsh said. "But he never acted on it since he was her boss before moving to Europol."

Sean set aside his mug and approached the table, shuffling papers and riffling through folders. "What did he find?"

"I'm still going through everything," Marsh said. "But it's less about the actual bombing or Eder's operations and more about finding the inside man."

"The inside man?" Levi set his teacup next to Sean's mug. "Someone at the Bureau on Eder's payroll? Besides Bell?"

"We didn't know about Bell until last month. Binny contended we should be looking for an Eder mole long before that. Someone at the embassy in Vienna or at one of the other agencies or organizations we worked with."

"Someone who fed Eder Sophie's location that night," Sean said.

"Someone," Marsh continued, "who knew who she was to our team and what would happen if they took her out. She held us together."

"My CI that night said it was an ISIS-affiliated group trying to make a statement," Sean reminded. "Maybe it wasn't about Sophie at all."

"Even I don't buy that," Levi said as he slumped into a chair. "There was a money trail back to Eder then, and now they've killed an SAC, tried to kill three other agents investigating them, and framed an ASAC." The lengths Eder would go to protect their criminal empire seemed endless.

Marsh squeezed his shoulder. "It's a billion-dollar operation. All of us running around with badges are small potatoes to Eder." He shot a smirk across the table. "Well, maybe not rich boy over there."

Sean shot him the bird. "You're one to talk."

Levi wished he could enjoy the banter between friends, but he was hung up on something Marsh had said earlier. "If Binny's believed this for a while, did your office pursue it earlier?"

Marsh lowered himself into the chair beside him. "We were looking into it, but then I stumbled onto your case, and the connections flashed like a neon sign. It seemed the faster route to shutting Eder down."

"Well, we're here now," Levi said as he ran a hand across Marsh's slumped shoulders. "We should investigate all routes."

"Agreed," Marsh and Sean both said, the latter following with, "Who were Binny's prime suspects?"

Marsh dragged the Binny box closer and pulled out a thin file. He tossed it across the table to Sean. "You, at one point."

"Me?"

"You bugged out in a hurry."

"Because my father was dying, and someone who shall remain nameless put me on the path back to my soul mates."

Marsh's *who me?* pose made Levi laugh. Even Sean, as tired as he obviously was, cracked a smile. The smiles faded, though, when Marsh pulled the two thickest files out of the box. He dropped the first one on the table. "Lennon Ross, FBI legal attaché in Vienna." Dropped the other file.

"Chief Inspector Theodore Wagner, our contact on the Austrian Federal Police in Vienna."

Sean slung his folder onto the table, his harsh actions and harsher "Fuck" telling Levi everything he needed to know. Their investigation had just taken a detour.

EIGHTEEN

LEVI STOOD in front of the gastropub, arms folded, staring at the sign over the door. "The Spyglass, really?"

"Ajay thinks he's funny," Marsh said.

"He is funny," Sean countered. "For a spook."

Marsh hooked an arm through Levi's, amused at the consternation that had taken up residence on his husband's face. The Hague was not turning out like Levi thought it would be at all. The Spyglass, though, Marsh could concede, was a conundrum. Eyes narrowed, lips pursed, Levi clearly couldn't make sense of the place. Not unlike Marsh's reaction the first time Sophie had brought him here. A seemingly odd choice for a spy's post-CIA career until you learned that everyone in global intelligence walked through those doors at some point.

Levi didn't buy it. "This is where you have top-secret meetings?"

"Would you believe treaties were negotiated here?" Marsh said. "Or information shared that brought down entire criminal empires?"

"Or the amount of money lost on World Cup betting?" Sean added.

"Now that I believe," Levi said with a laugh.

Laughed more as Marsh tugged him toward the door. "Think of it like Mos Eisley Cantina but on the North Sea and decked out in KNVB orange and cheesy nautical kitsch." It was eclectic, it was loud, and it hummed with energy and espionage. Two words that might as well have been stamped on Ajay Patel's forehead.

"Well, if it isn't the happy couple!" Ajay ducked under the bar flip and barreled toward them, the opposite of Binu in almost every way. Shorter, rounder, balder, and dressed in cargo shorts and a Van Dijk jersey. "I cannot believe you got hitched!" he said as he folded Marsh into a backslapping hug.

"Yoo-hoo." Sean waved from beside them, waggling his ring finger in Ajay's face. "I did too."

Ajay drowned him in a hug too, and Sean completely failed at playing offended, laughing as he returned the embrace. "We always knew you would, pretty boy, and you got two. Scorchers, I hear. But this one"—he slapped Marsh's shoulder—"we didn't have high hopes for him, but damn." He whistled as his dark gaze swept over Levi. Marsh would've been worried if he didn't already know Ajay was happily married. Didn't stop him from looking and appreciating, though. "You did good, Cowboy."

"I know I did." Marsh slid a hand into the groove of Levi's lower back. "Ajay Patel, my husband, Agent Levi Bishop. Levi, this is Ajay."

"It's a pleasure to meet you," Levi said, hand extended.

Ajay wrapped it in his bear paw and yanked Levi into a hug too. "All mine, Levi." He drew back, smiling wide.

"There's a bottle of Bollinger and a stiff fellow of absolutely no relation to me whatsoever waiting for you on the peak. Go on up, toast, enjoy, and I'll be up in a few with some eats."

As quickly as he'd come, Ajay bustled off, shouting a Dutch greeting at someone else who'd walked through the door. Levi's confused face returned, and Marsh couldn't help but laugh.

"That guy was CIA?"

"Some of the best spies are the loud ones. Folks never suspect them. Ajay uses all that commotion as cover."

"And he could talk to a tree," Sean added. "Or get blood from a stone."

Marsh led them through the restaurant, past the open-air patio, into the kitchen, and through the pantry, accessing a door hidden behind the shelves.

At the landing halfway up the flight of stairs, Levi ran his fingers over the painting on the wall, a nautical wheel with unusual detail inside the circle. "These are target crosshairs, aren't they?"

Marsh waggled his brows. "Maybe."

Levi rolled his eyes and followed Sean up the stairs, their group emerging onto the roof. The large square area with its glass walls was a widow's peak of sorts but with more sharp edges and less antebellum flourishes. It had the view, though, and a ghost haunting its perimeter. Binny paced along the seaside edge, shoulders slumped and face downturned, his hands in his pockets, the day's coat and tie long gone.

"Hey, boss," Sean said.

Binny jolted, chin and gaze jerking up, a clue as to just how far away in his thoughts he'd been. "I'm surprised you came," he said with a weak smile. "I thought once you saw your file you wouldn't be so friendly."

"It was a fair consideration. And a much smaller file than the others."

"Which we need to talk about," Marsh said.

"Can we toast first?" Binny gestured at the champagne and glasses on the low square table between the four rooftop loungers. "I didn't get the chance to properly congratulate you yesterday."

Marsh was right. The Binu who'd greeted them at the embassy was not the same Binny Marsh had worked beside. Today's Binny was more in line with the agent and boss he knew, polite and mannered with some of his usual stiffness exhausted out of him. Marsh tossed his Stetson on a lounger. "Lunchtime booze?"

"I'm taking the rest of the day off." Binny filled glasses and held the first out to Levi. "It's a pleasure to meet you, Levi, truly." He passed around the rest of the drinks, saluting Sean and Marsh with "Congratulations" before returning his attention to Levi. "You know he's a handful, right?"

"I'm learning." His smile said he enjoyed the lessons.

Marsh would take that. Would take more champagne too if Binny didn't finish it all himself, pouring his third glass before anyone else had had a second. "Long week?"

"Long month." He sank onto one of the loungers. "Long three years if we're all being honest."

Sean claimed the seat across from him and moved Marsh's hat out of the way. "So talk to us."

Marsh sat between them on the lounger that was perpendicular, Levi at his side. "When did you start back down the rabbit hole?"

"When you left for San Diego," Binny replied. "I couldn't sit here and do nothing." Because that torch he'd carried for Sophie still burned; now for justice. "I'm right that Eder has help. There's no way they get away with all they do without cover."

"Rep Anthony in the US."

"And Bell, my late SAC," Levi said.

"They can't be the only two." Binny raked a hand through his thick black hair, sunlight catching the silver strands, even more numerous than Marsh had noticed under the embassy's lights. "There has to be someone on this side of the pond too. Someone who allows them to operate unchecked in Austria and across Europe."

Marsh didn't disagree, but the proposition didn't exactly line up with Binny's casework. "That's more juice than Ross or Wagner have."

"But one or the other is a convenient first line of defense."

"Like Bell was," Levi said. "It's consistent, a mirror setup, same as they did their operations and money in Europe and the US." He shifted his attention squarely to Binny. "How certain are you that Sophie was the target? Sean's CI said it was about ISIS wanting to make a statement. Are you sure it wasn't about creating a bigger scene on the night of the benefit close-by the opera house?"

It was smart of him to ask, the outsider coming new to the case, he could get away with it. Marsh was equally curious as to Binny's thinking on the point. The CI's original information was the easiest solution. But easy solutions were rarely the answer.

"We can't be one hundred percent positive," Binny said. "I can't even be fifty percent in this case, but given Eder's latest course of action in San Diego—eliminating or discrediting anyone who might put the pieces together and finally nail them—it seems to fit."

Before anyone else could weigh in, the rooftop door banged open, Ajay coming through with a serving tray balanced on his shoulder. "I come bearing gifts." Marsh stood and helped him unload the tray. He wasn't lying about the gifts. Fresh fried samosas, a giant serving dish of steaming biryani, sides of salan and raita, and a basket of fresh naan. Marsh's mouth watered. The last good Indian food he'd had was in San Francisco in December, and even that was no comparison to the Patel family recipes. These were dishes that never made it out to the restaurant proper but often found their way upstairs to this table, secret food shared as secrets of a different sort flowed.

Ajay sat next to Binny. "It's goat. Your favorite. I expect you to eat two bowls of it. No argument."

Binny patted his knee. "You're a good older brother."

Levi was loading his plate too, the most food Marsh had seen him eye since leaving San Diego. "No more wooziness or nausea?"

"I'm back at sea level," he said around a bite of samosa. "I'm a happy seal again."

Marsh chuckled. "He didn't do too well in the Texas desert," he explained to the others.

"Fuck elevated deserts," Ajay concurred. "Never been sicker than when I was stationed in Pakistan. Months on end of altitude sickness."

Levi shook his head. "Four days and I wanted to die."

They continued to eat and make small talk until halfway into the second bottle of Bollinger when a lull in the conversation provided an opening back to their earlier conversation. "You helped him gather the info?" Marsh asked Ajay.

"Off the books."

"And what's your assessment?"

"Wagner," Ajay said at the same time Binny said, "Ross."

The table was too far away, so Marsh banged his head on Levi's shoulder instead. "Not helpful, guys."

Quiet laughs all around but Marsh was getting impatient. They'd been here a day too long already. What about this case was worth a spymaster's input? He needed to know. But he wanted to hear the lawyer's case first. "Ross, go," he prompted Binny.

"He was pissed. He was passed over for Europol. He was passed over for The Hague. And then Sophie brought the TOC mission to his jurisdiction, interfering there."

"He's still in Vienna?" Levi asked.

Marsh and Binny nodded.

"Why does he keep getting passed over?"

"He's not a political player," Ajay ventured.

"Or," Binny countered, "he's comfortable in Vienna taking Eder's money. Sophie and her team there would've made things very uncomfortable."

Marsh threw out another alternative that came to mind. "Or Ross's wife is independently wealthy, so he doesn't actually have to try that hard." Not everyone who was rich worked as hard as Sean to put their wealth to good use.

"Ross should've been on that train with her," Binny said. "I keep coming back to that."

Marsh had revisited that fact countless times himself since that night three years ago.

"Why wasn't he?" Levi asked.

"He took a car service," Binny answered.

"Which was not uncommon," Sean reminded them. "He did that a lot. Money and all."

"Speaking of money," Marsh said, "I saw in the files where you'd flagged several deposits into his brokerage account."

"Larger than usual sums but they usually fell right around tax time. Could just be tax planning," Ajay said. "I hit a brick wall trying to trace them further. I've still got some red tape on my heels."

With Ajay's connections, it must have been a pretty steep barrier. But Marsh had an ace up his sleeve. "I know a guy without any." He scratched a call to Holt onto his mental to-do list. "All right, that's Ross. Give me Wagner."

"He was your counterpart with the Federal Police in Vienna. He had the tech know-how and capabilities and all the information at his fingertips." Binny polished off another glass of Bollinger while his brother carried on. "He's also got an extended network of contacts from his time with the RAF, and he's a British ex-pat with no loyalty."

Sean gestured at Ajay. "You're a fucking ex-pat."

"And married to a Dutchwoman. I've got connections here. He's got none to Austria."

"Wagner is married," Marsh reminded.

"To another British ex-pat," Ajay shot back.

"He also plays chess," Binny added. "And introduced you to the craftsman who made your chess set."

Beside Marsh, Levi gasped. Inside Marsh, something in his chest clenched. "I don't think it's Wagner."

"You don't want it to be Wagner," Sean said quietly.

The entire table went silent, same as Marsh. He stared at

the sea, refusing to believe the friend he trusted was a traitor while knowing he had to fucking consider it. "Anything else on Wagner?"

"Financially, he's clean," Ajay said. "I'm still looking into his husband. He's an interior designer. His income is widely erratic. It's hard to tell what's out of the usual course and what isn't."

"Any connections to Eder?" Levi asked.

"Besides Catherine Sanders also being based out of the UK, nothing yet."

Yet. Always yet. For as long as they'd been working this case, for as much as they knew already, as much as they had discovered and solved for, the things they hadn't solved for yet seemed as endless as the sea beyond the plate-glass wall.

Levi settled a hand on his thigh, squeezing gently, trying to ease his mounting frustration. Marsh covered his hand and focused on the most immediate *yet* they needed to solve for, the primary reason they were here, their foothold for jurisdiction.

"Were you able to find anything on Stefan Sanders?" After their meeting with Binny at the embassy and after digging through his files last night, recognizing Ajay's prints all over his brother's off-book investigation, Marsh had reopened a secure line of communication with Ajay and asked him to do a sweep through intelligence channels for the Eder king's nephew.

"No record of him reentering the country. But—"

"They traffic folks for a living, I know."

"So we assume he's in Vienna?" Levi said.

"Not so fast." Ajay pulled a minitablet from one of his cargo short pockets and set it on the table so they all could see the screen. "The Sanders property in Salzburg is buzzing." He pressed Play on the paused black-and-white video and long-range surveillance showed a minicastle on a hill overrun with people, dashing every which direction, many of them with tablets in hand like the one Ajay was using.

"Salzburg?" Levi said. "I thought he was—we were—going to Vienna."

"Eder's corporate offices are in Vienna," Sean said. "But the family compound is in Salzburg."

"Where Catherine Sanders flew into this morning," Ajay said. "Her we have a record of." He pressed Play on a different black-and-white surveillance video, Catherine embracing two people outside the terminal entrance. "Her parents," Ajay supplied. "They flew in from the US."

"The ones estranged from Catherine's uncle?"

Binny nodded. "And they're on the guest list for a benefit Eder is hosting at the compound next weekend."

"That's why it's buzzing," Sean said.

Marsh's brain sped into hyperdrive, mentally reworking their game plan to cover two cities and two sites. They needed to go to Vienna to meet with Ross and Wagner, to work other aspects of the investigation. But if they were going to find Stefan Sanders, he'd put all his money on both Sanders heirs making an appearance at that benefit in Salzburg. Which meant only one thing. "We need in."

NINETEEN

THEY STAYED at the Spyglass through the afternoon and into the early evening, strategizing and discussing next steps on how to continue skirting the jurisdictional guidelines they were already flaunting before devolving into war stories told over fried everything from the bar menu downstairs—kroket, bitterballen, patat, and poffertjes. If not for their scheduled calls home, Binny's drooping eyelids, and the ritual evening summer storm, they'd probably still be there, eating too much and placing bets on a sport Marsh would never understand. And never call football. He was from Texas after all.

He slid open the balcony door and joined Levi in the soupy night air. The humidity didn't seem to bother Levi, who was lounging in one of the metal deck chairs. "Sean out?" he asked.

Twisting his torso, Marsh peeked inside to where Sean was asleep on the sofa bed. Sean had sold his place in town when he'd moved back to the States, and Paxton Industries didn't have an office here. He'd offered to stay at a hotel, but seeing as they were going to crash at Sean's place in Vienna, it was only fair Sean crashed here at his. And it made Marsh feel better to know his best friend was safe under the same roof. "Out like a light." He sank into the chair beside Levi's. "He's effectively working two jobs. Add in today's Indian buffet and fried feast…"

Levi billowed his shirt. "I can smell the oil and spices seeping out of my pores."

"We can go inside to the bedroom"—Marsh waggled his brows—"if it's too steamy out here."

"Then it'll be steamy in there, and we've got a houseguest."

Marsh scooted his chair closer, leaned over the arm, and grabbed his husband by the shirt front, hauling him closer. "Come here." He brought their lips together in a kiss that at any other time, without a houseguest and without all that food in their bellies, would have led directly to the bedroom. "This place isn't so bad with you around."

"Thanks. I think." He slumped back into his seat. "But I don't want to live here either."

"Agree." Marsh liked it well enough when he'd been running from sand and sun, but he wasn't like Binny. He didn't want to live here in the past with ghosts and bureaucratic red tape. Not when a life in the present, in a place and with people that felt like home already, was so close to becoming a reality. "We need to call David."

When they did, it wasn't David who picked up the phone. Camilla's face filled the screen instead. "Your son is helping Irina birth baby goats. Look!"

She flipped the phone, and sure enough, David was kneeling in a pasture in front of one of the breeding goats who was lying on her side. In his arms was a small ball of brownish-red baby goat. He held it in front of the mother, encouraging her to lick and clean her newborn while Irina worked to deliver another behind her.

"Number two is almost here," Irina called, and after an endless couple minutes, the second baby was clear, that one mostly white with a few brown spots. "It's a boy." Irina brought him around front and let David suction out its nose and mouth, then encourage the mother to claim her kid while Irina helped her finish pushing out the placenta.

"Hey, David," Camilla called. "Give your Dad and Marsh a smile."

He turned his head, and Marsh actually startled. He'd never seen a grin that big on David's face. "Look!" He shifted so they could see both babies, their mother fully engaged now with David's help. He scratched between her ears. "You did good, Belle."

"Good job!" Levi said from beside Marsh, and if the catch in his voice didn't give away his emotions, the tears in his eyes and the wobble of the phone did. He clicked the Mute button. "He looks so happy. I haven't seen him smile that big since..." His words trailed off, caught behind another lump, and Marsh curled an arm around his shoulders, holding him close and holding the phone with him. Levi's lips brushed his jaw, his choked words Marsh's heart. "Thank you."

"I've got it." Irina knelt beside David. "Go clean up so you can talk to them."

David disappeared offscreen, and Camilla flipped the phone back around. "He's a natural with the animals."

Levi wiped his eyes. "He always has been. They call him the dog whisperer in the neighborhood."

David appeared on-screen beside Camilla. "I think I

might want to do this. The vet thing. Can we talk about it when you two get home?"

Marsh jolted again, David's words fueling that fiery hope that continued to build inside him. Both these incredible men expected him to be there in San Diego, part of their family when this was all over.

Levi leaned more heavily into his side. "Of course."

"I'll get him up to speed," Irina called from somewhere close by, off camera. "Camilla, can I get a hand?"

She blew them a kiss goodbye and dropped a straw hat onto David's head. "Leave this on, or you'll become even more of a lobster."

She moved off in the direction of Irina's voice, leaving just David on-screen, leaning back against a fence post. "How's The Hague?"

"Very brick," Levi said. "And almost as red as you."

Marsh rolled his eyes. "Ignore him."

"And damp."

"But you're good? Safe?"

"We're good, David," Marsh said. "Headed to Vienna tomorrow."

The next step they'd decided on before leaving the Spyglass. Binny would stay and hold down The Hague front with Ajay while he, Sean, and Levi went to Austria. Vienna first to make contact with Ross and Wagner, snoop around Eder HQ, then get into that benefit in Salzburg. Sean was reluctant to flash his money, but if that's what it took, if Marsh needed to throw around some of his too, he'd do it, so long as the money was redirected before it ever hit Eder's pockets.

"And you'll be safe there?" David asked again.

"Sean's family owns a building downtown," Levi explained. "We'll be staying there with added security."

David's eyes grew wide. "They own the building? How the hell am I ever gonna lure Trevor away from him?"

Levi shook his head, laughing, and Marsh thought maybe best not to crush the poor kid's dreams by telling him the Paxtons owned the entire block of buildings. And that no one was ever luring Trevor away from Sean and Charlie again. "I rewired the entire security system myself last year when he took over."

David nodded, seemingly reassured.

"Did you get the picture I sent?" Levi asked.

"That didn't look like brick."

"The coast is pretty. Tell us about the rest of your day."

They settled in, listening as David animatedly told them about monitoring Belle's vitals and behavior as she'd ambled about all morning, grazing, until settling down in one corner of the pasture.

"David! House now! Please!" called a high-pitched, trilling voice. Lily demanding his presence, her next words making clear why. "Mama Milla says snack time."

"You heard the boss lady."

It was David's turn to roll his eyes. "You have no idea."

"Hey, David." Levi called his attention back to them, much less earsplitting than Lily but still effective. "I'm proud of you."

"And if the vet thing is what you want," Marsh said, "we'll make it happen."

His broad smile returned, and Marsh snapped a screenshot before they ended the call.

"You mean that?" Levi said as Marsh handed the phone back to him.

"Anyone who finds the thing they love, that thing they want to spend the rest of their life doing, is lucky, and to find it that young, that's a gift. We should encourage it."

Levi's smile was almost as bright as his son's. "We? You believe that now? You'll be with us?"

He palmed the back of Levi's head and drew him closer, dropping a kiss on his forehead. Breathing in the fresh, peppermint-tinged scent he wanted to spend the rest of his life this close to. "I'm trying to, Levi. I want to more than anything."

Levi tilted his face and returned the kiss squarely on Marsh's lips. "We'll keep giving you reasons to believe."

TWENTY

"WHAT DO YOU SEE?"

"The place where your friend died." Levi had studied the crime scene photos from three years ago and watched the surveillance video of the subway platform and surrounding area more times than Marsh knew, trying to find some way to contribute, to bring Marsh peace.

Of course he'd recognize the square where Sean had dropped them off. The reflecting pool, the giant baroque church with its green dome, the university and museum buildings on either side of the square, the blue U signs that led to where they stood now, inside the massive underground transit station where Sophie and nine other people had lost their lives.

"Tell me exactly what you see."

They started on the U4 green line, the platform where the explosion had taken place. They walked it like a crime scene, noting distances to the escalators at either end of the platform, to the train Sophie had stepped off, the number of lights and surveillance cameras, Marsh pointing out the existing versus new ones that were added after the attack. Counting heads in evening rush-hour traffic. They did the same for the U1 red and U2 purple lines that also ran through Karlsplatz station, then also for the winding underground shopping area between the U-Bahn lines and the surface.

"Walk me around the above-ground access points," Levi said once he'd seen enough below.

Marsh smirked. "This is why I had Sean go ahead in the car with the bags."

With the rush-hour crowd, it took extra time to do a thorough walk around, finishing at the vine-covered entry below the historic station building. "This place is huge," Levi said.

When Marsh didn't reply, Levi turned to find him standing several feet away next to a landscaped bed of flowers, his eyes glued to a bronze plaque that stood knee-high, raised enough to be noticed but not obtrusively so. Closing the distance, reading the plaque, Levi understood Marsh's silence and observed the same.

Ten victims' names, including Sophie Cohen.

He stepped behind Marsh and looped his arms around his waist, hugging him from behind. "Even if Sean had gotten to you sooner, neither of you could have stopped this. You know that, right?" Having walked the site himself, Levi better understood the impossibility. Without more precise advance intel, there would have been no telling which of the above-ground entrances Peter Bauer would've used, which line he would've targeted, which escalator or stairs he would've taken down to the platform. It hurt Levi's heart that Marsh had struggled with his guilt for as long as he had. He offered what absolution he could. "I know what you want me to say, but you didn't miss anything. You couldn't have guessed at this. The fact you and Sean pieced together where to look that fast was remarkable."

Marsh's hands covered his and held them flat against his chest. "We shouldn't have had to guess. We should have had the surveillance."

"You were locked out of the surveillance. Who do you think engineered that? Wagner? Ross? Anthony?"

"Eder, one way or the other."

"We'll get them." He hugged Marsh tighter. "We'll get justice for her and everyone else whose name is on that plaque. I promise."

TWENTY-ONE

LEVI COULDN'T GET ENOUGH of the rooftops and balconies in Europe. The view was so different from what he was used to. Yes, they had a great one from their backyard in San Diego, but the North Sea from Marsh's apartment, the sea and the city from atop the Spyglass, and now the steeples of St. Stephen's Cathedral from the rooftop patio of Sean's penthouse in Vienna were like no vista he'd ever seen.

The patio doors opened, and a barefoot Marsh, hair still wet from their shower, stepped out onto the roof. Levi rested back against the balcony wall. "The penthouse? How rich is Sean?"

"Very."

"He doesn't seem it."

Marsh raised a brow.

"Okay, there are certain clues if you pay attention." The expensive haircut, the understated tailored clothes, the private jet and private cars when they saved time. But there was no fancy jewelry or other look-at-me-I'm-rich annoyances. "He's not flashy about it, though."

"Ask him to tell you his story." Marsh leaned beside him. "Both sets of parents who raised him were good people. He's good people."

"He's risking a lot helping us. Charlie too."

"It's what friends do."

"It's been a minute."

Marsh didn't need to raise a brow, his searching stare question enough. Gentler too as if he realized the sensitive spot he'd nudged. Levi rested his forearms on the balcony rail, looking out and looking in, considering anew the past two years. "After Kristin died, I withdrew from everything but work and family. She was the social one, the life of the party, not me. Most of our friends were kid adjacent, other parents we met in the neighborhood or at this or that school function or sporting event. I lost touch..." He hadn't returned their phone calls after the funeral, hadn't reached out to reconnect, hadn't volunteered at school or on the field like Kristin used to bargain with him to do. She'd enjoyed it, being around people, and Levi hadn't realized until now much he'd enjoyed it too, missed it even. "Being around folks again, in more than just a work capacity, is good. It's good for David too." His engaged interactions with Holt, Brax, and Lily, his hilariously dramatic fascination with the trio, the way he'd taken to Camilla, Irina, and Mi Herencia. "I didn't realize how much we'd both been hiding in our caves."

Marsh bumped his hip. "I'd like to meet some of them when we get home. I'll make Frito pie for the PTA meetings."

"Hell no on the pie, but I like the 'we' talk." Liked the

taste of it even more, the future on Marsh's lips brushing his.

"If you two newlyweds are done canoodling," Sean called from behind them, "we've got a status check in fifteen. And lunch is served."

Levi hummed against Marsh's mouth. "Lunch sounds good." They reluctantly ceased their canoodling and followed Sean inside, loading their plates with schnitzel, potato salad, and white asparagus. "So the massive lunchtime meal wasn't just a Netherlands thing?"

"Nope," Marsh said. "Lunch is the biggest meal here too."

"I could ask the staff to just leave out cold cuts for lunch," Sean said, "but we'd end up with the entire deli case."

Levi settled at one end of the table. "I think I like it here."

"You like that you can eat again. Bottomless pit like your kid."

David did come by it honestly. Levi was just grateful he could hold down food again. All of it was delicious, and thank fuck for the computer ping as they finished up or else it would have been impossible to fend off the food coma. Sean answered the ping, displaying the multiparty video call on the wall-mounted big screen across from the table. Places and faces filled the boxes, the most welcome a familiar one at the head of the table in the FBI San Diego war room. "Ma'am," Levi greeted his ASAC.

"Aren't we past that, Levi?" Kwan replied.

Julia didn't work in his mind, so he tried, "Kwan."

"Better," she said with a nod, then let them have it. "And fuck you both for not already having this locked down by the time I got sprung. I expected more from you."

Marsh smirked. "Good to see jail didn't change you, Eagle."

Levi, though, failed to find the humor in the situation. "You're not pissed about the jail time?"

"It wasn't pleasant," she answered. "But better someone try to frame me than blow me up."

"Silver lining," Matt said from her right.

"Plus, my attorney was hot as fuck."

Matt replicated his full body shiver from several days ago again, and in his Texas screen square, Holt nearly spit out his soda.

"Are you officially back at work?" Marsh asked Kwan.

"Still technically suspended." She swung her gaze to Byrne on her other side.

"OPR doesn't work as fast as the rest of the legal system," he replied.

"So put me to work," she said to them. "I've got time on my hands and the hot blond was married, so I need to drown my single sorrows in something productive."

It was more than Levi had ever heard his ASAC divulge about her personal life. Had jail changed her? Or was it just working with old colleagues that had loosened her up? Either way, he'd take all the help they could get. Marsh was also on board, the two of them, plus Sean, bringing everyone else up to speed on the latest intel.

"If Ross or Wagner is the Bell there," Cam said, "who's the Anthony?"

"And is Anthony working with that person?" Sean said.

"I want on that," Kwan said. "I need to know who set me up, and I've got the connections to help work it."

Charlie and Cam offered to officially liaise while Matt smartly deferred, that inquiry above his pay grade.

"Any leads on the chess boxes?" Levi asked. They were the most concrete pieces of evidence they had.

"About that," Holt said as he shared his screen, familiar footage from outside Kwan's office the night of the attacks on pause. "This is ultimately why the charges were dropped." He hit Play, and if Levi hadn't seen the video himself, he would never believe it. At the point the footage previously cut off, it continued to play now, showing a janitor removing the box from Kwan's office and handing it to none other than SAC Bell.

Levi propped both elbows on the table, hands framing his *Home Alone* face. "He stole the box that ultimately blew him up?"

Cam nodded. "Brax tracked down the janitor in Boca. He took a vacation with the five grand Bell paid him. Also turns out he opened it before handing it off to Bell. Nothing happened."

Kwan connected the dots. "Proving I didn't rig it before it was out of my possession."

"Who'd he hand it off to?" Sean asked.

"Working on that now," Matt said. "But take a stab at my top three guesses."

Marsh ticked them off. "Anthony. Anthony. Anthony."

"Bingo!"

"Did he think he was setting you up?" Levi said to Kwan.

"Probably, that asshole."

"What about the box that was sent to Matt?" Marsh asked.

"Forensics managed to salvage a portion of a logo from

a piece that wasn't blown to bits," Matt said. Holt stopped screen sharing so Matt could share his, snapshots on display.

"That's an edelweiss in the center," Sean said.

"And is that the Prater Ferris wheel around the outside?" Marsh added. "The box maker is here?"

"Yep." Matt flipped to the next photo, the full crest appearing. "We traced the logo to a Harald Pincler. He has a small carpentry shop in an area called Grinzing. Ring any bells?"

"The area, yes," Sean said. "It's where a bunch of the local wineries are in the hills north of the city. As for the craftsman, that name is new to me." He looked to Marsh. "What about you?"

Marsh shook his head. "New to me too. Not the same person who made mine and Kwan's. We'll check it out here on the ground," he told the team.

Levi continued ticking off the open leads in his head. "What about Greg and Amanda?"

"Still in the wind," Matt replied. "But you were right about giving the potential victims time."

"You've got something?"

"Amanda mentioned another possible location to one of the women. Out in Poway. Will and Alyssa are on their way there to check it out now."

"I'm running down the ownership records," Holt said, beating Levi to his next question.

"Gail also reached out to Amanda on a personal email address. We'll see if she bites."

"Anything else?" Marsh said.

"Something even better." Matt rubbed his hands together, looking entirely too gleeful for having been recently concussed. "JoJo was outside Greg's shelter office when she overheard a call between Greg and a British-sounding woman."

"Catherine Sanders?" Sean posited. "She was schooled and works in London."

"Likely," Holt said, then ran a clip of her speaking at a charity event last year. "JoJo took a listen too and thinks it's the same person."

"What did Catherine say?" Marsh asked.

"She was threatening to foreclose on the building," Matt relayed, "if Greg didn't deliver the merchandise." The last two words were a sneer, all the good-natured agent's affability gone.

"We already pulled the building records for the shelter," Cam said. "Not Eder, Orchard, or any affiliate we have record of."

"It has to be connected to Eder and Orchard," Levi said to those around the table and on-screen. Someone was pulling levers, and this was obviously one of them.

Marsh delivered an interesting twist. "Or Catherine is playing her own game."

TWENTY-TWO

AS MUCH AS Marsh enjoyed a cold bottle of Modelo on a hot afternoon or an Anchor Steam while cruising the foggy Bay, there was also something special about a stein of Gosser after work, sipped in the corner booth of his favorite pub in Vienna. Close to the embassy, Below Ground was a favorite haunt of their legat team. In one of the neobaroque buildings near Liechtensteinpark, the light wood furnishings and sidewalk-level transoms gave the subbasement space a new and bright feel despite the centuries-old structure. And the cozy comfort food dishes that came out of the kitchen were to die for.

Tonight, there was an equally scrumptious dish at the bar.

Marsh sipped from his beveled mug and eyed the blond bombshell. A little over six feet, the man's hair was damp, the fresh short undercut dark, the longer top strands drying to dark blond. His charcoal tee showed off broad shoulders and a V-shaped torso, lean muscles Marsh could spend days running his lips and hands over, and when he was done showering the man's back with affection, he'd peel down the dark denim and plant his face in the crack of his firm, round ass. But as tempting as the man's backside was, it was nothing compared to the bright blue eyes that met Marsh's in the backbar mirror.

That invited closer inspection.

Sean shifted in the booth beside Marsh and laid his phone, screen down, on the table. "Quit ogling your husband."

Marsh winked at Levi. Levi winked back. "My flirt muscles were getting rusty."

"He's supposed to be working. So are you."

Marsh flagged down the passing server. "Would you mind getting my friend here another beer?"

"I'm fine," Sean said with a polite smile, then once the server laughed and moved on, asked Marsh, "Are you sure this is the best idea? Meeting Wagner and Ross together?"

"We play them off each other. See if either flinches or if they've been working together since we left." He cut a glance to the bar. "And Levi over there is our impartial observer." With an earpiece that allowed him to hear every word they were saying. "Less likely to spook them too, new face and all." He was hoping that wouldn't matter, that Binny and Ajay were wrong, but the Patels were too good at their jobs to dismiss the possibility. Any lead was worth following under the current circumstances.

"Showtime," Levi radioed, and Marsh swung his gaze to the door.

"Entering together," Sean observed as Ross held the door open for Wagner.

"Or maybe they're both just prompt." Marsh followed

Sean out of the booth, standing beside the table and flagging down their colleagues.

"Well, well, well," Wagner said in his familiar Cockney accent. "Look what the cat dragged in." Marsh could say the same about Wagner. His blond hair was shaggy and curling on the ends, and the bags under his eyes were almost as dark as the indigo of his eyes.

"Couldn't stay away," Marsh said, shaking his hand.

Ross tossed his trench into the booth. "Or you've got nothing better to do while you're suspended."

"Suspended?" Wagner's shock seemed genuine, his gaze bouncing between the two of them.

Ross, however, had moved on to greeting—needling—Sean. "Or while you're running a corporate empire."

Sean shrugged, then slid into the booth. "Old habits die hard."

Marsh caught the attention of the server again, ordered a round of drinks for the table, then after a quick glance Levi's direction, claimed the end of the booth beside Sean. "How are you two?"

"Overworked," Wagner said.

Ross loosened the paisley tie around his neck, corded muscles under his dark skin flexing. "Same story, different agency."

"Do you get the chance to work together much?" Sean asked.

"With you two gone, Binny's drawn back." Marsh detected disappointment in the Virginian's voice. "Lack of resources and warm bodies. We'll have the occasional joint op, but without your TOC task force, those usually run through Europol or the CIA."

"Anything else from our Balkan friends?" Marsh asked.

It was a lead they couldn't forget about. It was the lead that technically gave them jurisdiction to hang their hat on, the FBI authorized to work with local authorities to combat global threats.

Which was why the Bureau had Ross, their legat in Vienna. "What part of suspended didn't you understand?"

"All of it."

Ross laughed, Wagner not so much. He was closer to the ground than Ross would ever be, and it had always been Marsh's impression that the chief inspector took his job personally, a calling versus a career. The primary reason he couldn't buy Wagner as Eder's mole. "There's always rumblings from those groups," the inspector said. "But they're mostly quiet these days. The system you built helps a lot. It gives us more eyes and ears and more lead time to stop incidents before they happen. If I never said thank you before, thank you. You've been more instrumental than you know."

"Good," Marsh said. He was frustrated it hadn't been enough, that it had been compromised the night of Sophie's death, but overall pleased that their work was making a positive difference. "That's why legats are here."

"Except the mission," Ross said, "doesn't feel nearly as on-mission these days."

"How so?"

"Without the TOC task force, without any task force for that matter, it's a scattershot approach at best. Crisis management versus a defined objective." He took a healthy swallow of his beer the server had dropped off. "It's exhausting and frustrating as hell." Disappointed, for sure, more so than Marsh expected. He wasn't buying Ross as the mole either. Neither Ross nor Wagner seemed happy with the Bureau's less involved approach.

"Any change in the major players here in Austria?" Sean asked. "Or in central Europe?"

"Oil and energy providers wield more power lately," Wagner said. "Otherwise, it's the usual criminal elements."

"And Eder Capital?"

"Still can't pin shit on 'em," Ross said, some of his Southern coming through. "Not for lack of trying, but they're as impenetrable as they've always been."

"What happened stateside?" Wagner asked.

"We shut their San Diego front down," Marsh answered.

"Then why the fuck are you suspended?"

"An SAC got killed in the process."

"Bloody hell, Marsh. It's never a dull moment with you."

"Aww, Wags." Marsh squeezed his hand where it rested on the table. "You sound like you missed me."

"I did."

Marsh drew his hand back, Wagner's response rawer than expected of a professional colleague. Levi must have noticed too, spinning on his stool like he was ready to come mark his territory.

No need.

Marsh rose and snagged the empties. "I'm going to get us a round of shots. Sounds like we need it." He carried the glasses to the bar and slid in next to Levi. "Easy, baby," he mumbled before ordering a round of Wild West shots from the bartender.

"You're going to explain that later," Levi said.

"Nothing to explain." Marsh sidled closer as he waited

for his drink order to be filled. "And you're the one I'm going home with tonight."

Levi checked the time on his phone. "We've got our call with David in an hour."

"We won't miss it." The bartender dropped off the small tray of shots, and Marsh picked it up and balanced it on one hand as he leaned closer to Levi. "In case you didn't know, you're the sexiest piece of ass in this joint."

That brought a smile to Levi's face, his eyes sparkling with confidence and challenge. "Enjoy your sugar shots."

Marsh smiled the entire way back to the table.

"I'd heard the rumors," Ross said as he passed out the shots. "And the ring says it's true, but that looked suspiciously like you flirting at the bar."

"I'm a happily married man. Was just letting him down easy."

Wagner deflated impossibly more, from *what the cat dragged in* to *the cat wouldn't even bother*. "So you're not back for good?"

Marsh shook his head. "I'll be moving to San Diego when this is all said and done."

Wagner heaved a sigh, then straightened and plastered on a smile. "All right, whatever I can do to help. You deserve to be happy." The sentiment seemed genuine and fit with everything Marsh knew and thought about Teddy Wagner, a decorated soldier and a good cop.

"Ross?" Sean prompted.

"There's only so much I can do under the Bureau's nose, but if I can help, count me in." Likewise consistent with Marsh's impression of their colleague.

"Well, then." Marsh raised his shot and clinked his glass

against the others'. "Since you're both so accommodating, which of you can get us tickets to the Eder benefit next week?"

Marsh was lucky he didn't take a whiskey shower.

TWENTY-THREE

THEIR NIGHTLY CALL with David ended in tears. Happy ones. David was still giddy over the birth of the new goats. He'd named the roan one Kristin and the spotted one Bond. Hence Levi's tears. Even Marsh's eyes were glassy. David had spent all day with the newborns, learning from Irina about their care and development from kids to adults. He was a teenager, and teens often changed their minds about the future, but David seemed to really love this. And Levi loved it for him. Loved Mar—

He cut short the thought, afraid to let the idea and words fully form, even as the truth burrowed deeper into his chest. Even as he planned a future with the man he leaned against, quiet as they contemplated the strides David was making, that they were making as a family, regardless of how their unit had come to be.

Eventually, the quiet moment was interrupted, Sean joining them in the living area with two coffees and a tea. "Will cut through the heavy stuff."

Levi detached himself from Marsh's side and laid a

hand over his belly, still full from the käsespätzle and apfel-strudel—mac and cheese, then apple strudel—he'd eaten at the bar while listening in on the four former colleagues catch up and strategize. "Metaphorical or physical?" he asked Sean.

The former agent's quiet laugh was perceptive like he'd known to give them time and that they'd need a distraction afterward. He was a good detective, even a year out from the Bureau. "Do you secretly hide out in Paxton's risk management department so you get to investigate still?"

"Me?" Sean hid a smile behind the rim of his mug. "Never."

"Got it. All the time, then." Everyone laughed, and Levi was reminded again how good it felt to spend time with friends. Hoped Sean and his family would visit them in San Diego when they weren't in the middle of a work shitstorm.

"You pick up anything tonight?" Sean asked.

"Other than the fact Wagner's interested in Marsh."

"He always was," Sean said, then to Marsh, "Did he ever act on it?"

Levi cut a sideways glance at Marsh. He wasn't letting him off this time. He expected an answer. "After you left," Marsh said to Sean. "We were working late one night, he made a pass at me, but that's as far as it went. I didn't recip-rocate. One, I wasn't interested in him like that, and two, he's married."

"Unhappily?" Levi asked. "I didn't see a ring on his finger."

"Very unhappily," Sean answered. "He and Philippe have been on the verge of divorce as long as we've known him."

"Still a no," Marsh said. "Too Catholic for that guilt. And the curse."

Sean narrowed his eyes. "What curse?"

"It's broken now," Levi answered, not giving his husband a moment's doubt. "How much did they know about Eder? Obviously, something. You mentioned it tonight, but were they fully read in?"

"They knew Eder was on our radar," Sean said. "More so after the explosion, as our investigation led that direction. But they didn't know as much as Binny."

Marsh sucked in a sharp breath, and Levi glanced between them. "Is Binny a suspect?"

"He had an alibi that night," Marsh said.

"Doesn't mean he didn't help set things in motion," Sean countered.

"He loved her."

"That sounds like more than a torch," Levi interjected.

"And she didn't return the feelings," Sean piled on. "He looked like hell."

"Because he's doing the work of three people."

"I know you like this less than Wagner and Ross, but it has to be considered."

Afraid this tennis match would go on for hours and recognizing the strain both Sean and Marsh were already under, Levi focused them back on the immediate suspects. "Putting Binny aside for now," he conceded, "what do you think between Ross and Wagner?"

"Ross," Marsh said at the same time Sean said, "Wagner," a hilariously spot-on impression of Binny and Ajay. Levi pretended to be Marsh and banged his head against his husband's shoulder.

Marsh chuckled. "What do you think?"

"I think we should wait to see what Ajay and Holt turn up on the bank accounts." There were discrepancies connected to both, and following the money had gotten them this far, had helped take down Eder's West Coast operation. They couldn't lose sight of what worked for them before, the financial and operational details that could take an empire down. But instincts played a role too. "But for what it's worth, I don't think Wagner would do that to you," he said to Marsh. "Ross had more to gain from the bombing and from Sophie's death."

"How so?" Sean prompted.

Levi was sure Sean saw it too—he was too good to miss the motive—but talking it out was also part of the process. "Professionally, she's out of his jurisdiction and he can direct the FBI's mission in Vienna however he sees fit, in Eder's favor or not. His play. And it sounds like he's operating unchecked."

"He could also coordinate with anyone else in the Bureau," Marsh said. "Like Bell stateside or someone else in the other legat offices."

"I don't actually think it's either of them," Levi said. "Yes, they both seem unhappy and overworked, but would they kill a colleague, risk innocent lives, risk their careers, and lose you two as friends?" He shook his head. "I don't see it."

"So we wait," Sean said.

"And meet with Charles Sanders."

Levi laughed at how fast Marsh's head whipped his direction. "What?"

Sean didn't bother to speak, just looked at him like he'd lost his mind, and maybe he had, but after that call with David, Levi was raring to move this forward, to get out of the corner they were stuck in and get home. To start living the life that was unspooling before him—with Marsh.

"It's a risk," he said, anticipating Marsh's first objection. "But we were planning to poke around Eder HQ anyway. They know we're here. Someone's told them, or they're monitoring us. We didn't fly in under fake documents."

"Probably both," Marsh conceded.

"So let's use your maneuver. Theoretical novelty. Something unexpected to put them off-balance, to flush them out."

Marsh cocked a brow. "That didn't go too well the last time."

"Liar!" Levi shoved his arm. "The first time, Bell, we assume, leaked the op info. Not your fault. The second time, we rescued five women."

"Do you really think this is the best idea?" Sean said, finally finding his words.

Marsh, though, was coming around to Levi's argument, catching on to where his brain was going. "He's right. They know we're here. And they know you're rich and out of the Bureau."

"They probably know you have money too," Levi said. "Me? Not a penny left until we married, but you two? You're big fish."

"And they think we're suspended."

Sean finally caught on. "You want them to think they can recruit us. Why would they believe that?"

"With limited exception"—Levi gestured at the two of them—"most rich people think they can buy anyone. They think other people just want to be rich too. They can make you richer, and they can add two more insiders to their stable of turncoats."

"Or think they can," Marsh said, "while we get the information we need."

"At a minimum, we get invites to the benefit. You have money. It'll look bad if they say no to potential donors."

"Nice work, Bishop."

"I've been learning about romantic chess from this guy."

"Ugh." Sean flapped a dismissive hand at them. "You're getting as nauseating as Holt and Brax."

"Says the guy I watched fall back in love with his soul mates last summer."

"Touché." Sean rose from the table. "Let me see what I can do on my end."

As he left the room, Marsh angled toward Levi. "You ready for this?"

"I'm ready for the after part." He leaned over and brushed his lips against his husband's. "With you."

TWENTY-FOUR

LEVI WAS MIXING drinks at the wet bar when Marsh crested the stairs to the penthouse's guest suite. He clicked his tongue against the back of his teeth, making a chiding sound. "You were a jock. Surely, you learned the saying in college…"

"Don't call me Shirley," Levi snarked, quoting one of his and David's go-to veg-out movies. Marsh chuckled; mission accomplished. "And yes, liquor before beer, never fear. Beer before liquor, never sicker. A rule that *you* broke at the pub." He popped the top on a bottle of ginger ale and split the soda between two glasses, pouring it over ice, grenadine, and lime. "Which is why we're drinking Shirley Temples." He stirred the drinks, tossed the bar spoon into the sink, and picked up the glasses. He headed to the bedroom, pausing over the threshold to glance back at Marsh, whose brows had drawn together in a confused expression. Good. Levi enjoyed knocking him for a loop every now and then, especially when his husband would enjoy the surprise. And Levi was certain he'd enjoy this one, ever since this idea had taken root at the pub, inspired by Marsh's own behavior. "You can leave your hat on," he said with a wink.

Marsh easily hit the softball, adjusting his Stetson and humming the tune as he followed Levi into the bedroom.

"I can play it on my phone," Levi said, "if you need it to recreate the mood."

Marsh kicked the door shut and leaned against it. "What mood?"

Levi crossed the room to the dresser with the mirror above it. He set the glasses down and lifted his gaze, meeting the reflection of Marsh's curious brown one. Good again. He was hooked; Levi just had to reel him into the fantasy. A little role play, a little time out of their heads and their chaotic world. "Two strangers in a pub. Been shooting eyes at each other all night. The one at the bar asks the bartender to pour two Manhattans." Levi pushed one of the glasses to his left and rested his forearms on the dresser, ass out in invitation. "He wants to see if the other guy will bite."

"Bite, huh?" Marsh pushed off the door and sauntered over. His eyes flicked to the drink. "You saving that for someone?"

"You."

Marsh went to remove his hat, and Levi hummed another few bars of the tune. Smirking, Marsh righted it on his head. "You want me to take off my coat and shoes? Go stand on a chair and shimmy?"

"Not yet," Levi said before taking a swallow of his drink.

Marsh did the same, then had the audacity to lick his lips. "You like cowboys?" he asked, as he lowered his glass.

"Not something you see around here every day."

Marsh's heated gaze raked over his body. He stepped closer, a scant inch between them. "Not every day someone as gorgeous as you walks into this pub either."

On the verge of combusting, Levi wanted to dive into Marsh's heat—desperately—but they were also having fun. They needed this, needed the light to balance the heavy. "Gorgeous, huh?"

"You know you are." He lifted a hand and carded his fingers through the flop of hair Levi couldn't keep out of his eyes since Camilla had cut it in Texas. "This hair." Drifted his hand lower, down his neck. "These shoulders." Traced the breadth of them, then journeyed down his spine. "Muscles down this perfectly V-shaped back." Palmed the cheek Levi had used to invite him over. "This glorious fucking ass."

"You're awfully forward."

"Says the man who lured me over here." He closed the remaining distance between them, hand palming Levi's other ass cheek, erection hard against Levi's hip. "Was there something else you wanted?"

"Your dick. In my ass."

Marsh laughed, the sexy rumble a cocktail Levi could drink all night long. "Now who's forward?" said the man running his hand along Levi's crack.

Levi tossed back the rest of his drink, set the glass aside, then took Marsh's left hand in his and placed it on his dick. "Forward and hard."

Groaning, Marsh melted against his side. "Jesus."

"Not Jesus, just Levi." He thrust into Marsh's hand. "Can you take care of this for me, Cowboy?"

Marsh shot out a hand, bracing himself against the

dresser behind Levi while he palmed Levi's length with the other. He nuzzled the side of his face, warm breath a river running behind Levi's ear and down his neck, turning up the heat in all the right places. "Oh, baby, I can take such good care of you." Another long, torturous stroke. "My apartment's just across the street. I can have my dick in that ass in less than five minutes. Railing you. Making you scream."

"Ten minutes," Levi countered. "I want the strip tease first. I want you naked, all but the hat. I want you on your knees, sucking me off, your own cock hard and dripping all over your thighs and the floor. Then I want you to rail me with that stiff, hot pri—"

"Deal." Marsh rotated in the blink of an eye, caging him against the dresser, chest to chest, claiming his mouth with brutal, delicious force. Negotiation over but the fantasy played on, Marsh trailing wet, open-mouthed kisses down his neck. "This is me shoving you up against the wall outside the pub because I cannot wait the thirty seconds it'll take to get into my apartment to taste you." He pressed their bodies together—chests, thighs, cocks. "Cannot wait for you to feel how hard I am already."

Levi grabbed his chin and hauled his mouth back to his, needing another taste, soaring higher with each nibble, each swipe, each thrust, their lower bodies rolling together. But they were flying too high too fast if Levi wanted that strip tease. He planted his hands on Marsh's chest and shoved him back. "Start stripping."

They were both panting too hard to hum much less sing, but Marsh slowly working his clothes off had the intended effect. By the time Marsh's jeans and boxers were gone, his shirt hanging open, Levi had his own jeans unbuttoned and a hand inside his boxers, alternately pumping his cock and grasping his balls to stave off his orgasm. Marsh peeled the shirt down his arms and tossed it aside, leaving him naked but for his hat. Exactly as Levi had asked, exactly how he wanted him. He stalked toward Levi while fisting his own plump cock, precome coating his fingers. "Is this what you wanted to see, Levi? How hard, how hot, I am for you?"

Levi tore his gaze from Marsh's cock and immediately second-guessed himself, this new sight far more erotic than the other. Marsh's face was etched in painful perfect desire, cheeks a red-stained bronze, pupils blown wide, lips wet and plump from the earlier savaging. Levi clasped his balls again, strangling the threatened climax and his words. "The stranger you just met in a bar?"

"No," Marsh growled. "My fucking husband." He grabbed Levi by the ass, lifted him, and dumped him onto the dresser. Tipped him back enough to rip his jeans and boxers off, righted him, then bent over his lap and swallowed his cock.

All the way to the back of his throat.

With his fucking hat still on.

Levi smacked the dresser with his open palm. "Fucking hell." Arched his back and thrust as Marsh's throat tightened around his tip. "Holy fuck." His legs tried to close, to lock Marsh's head in a vise he could never escape because ohmigod his hot, wet mouth—that suction—around his dick was divine, but Marsh flattened his hands against his inner thighs and spread him open, making room to bob on his cock with the occasional detour to his balls and taint, spit dribbling south, so close to where Levi needed this to go. He scooted forward and lifted his hips. Reading him right, Marsh dropped the rest of the way to his knees, draped Levi's legs over his shoulders, and dragged his ass to the edge of the dresser. Wide open, hole on display, Marsh took advantage, tongue teasing his rim, paving the way for his spit-slick fingers, working him open.

Hat teetering.

Levi grabbed it, shoved it on his own head, and Marsh's leather and tea tree oil scent invaded his senses. Overloaded the circuit as Marsh stroked his cock and penetrated deep with three fingers. Levi bucked, coming hard, soaking his own T-shirt and Marsh's fist with come.

Marsh, however, was far from done with him. He rose, all of him rosy and hard, and grasped Levi's wrist, hauling him upright. He plucked off the Stetson, tossed it onto the corner chair, then rid Levi of his shirt, discarding it in the pile of clothes on the floor. Then, same as Levi had done earlier, Marsh guided Levi's hand to his erection. "I'm dripping, just like you wanted."

Levi slumped against his chest, forehead on his sweaty shoulder, as he stroked Marsh's cock. "I need this—you—inside me."

"You still want me to rail you?"

Levi tipped back his head, smiling. Blissed out, loose, ready and willing to be used. "Show me how happily married you are."

"Challenge accepted." Marsh yanked him off the dresser, carried him to the bed, and a generous squirt of cool lube massaged into his worked-open hole later, drove into him in one single, brutal thrust.

Back bowed, Levi pressed his head back into the pillow, eyes screwed shut, stars exploding behind his lids. "Holy fuck." More as Marsh set a brutal pace, the railing he promised, that Levi continued to beg and plead for. "Harder, harder."

Sitting back on his haunches, Marsh jerked him onto his lap and pumped up, the penetration so deep it brought tears to Levi's eyes. Brought him to the edge again. His hole clenched around Marsh's cock, and with a strangled grunt, Marsh spilled into him, filled him up, his hands splayed under his back, head to his chest, murmuring Spanish bene-dictions as they drifted in bliss together, as they sank to the bed, a sated tangle of limbs, a blanket of warmth in and around Levi.

He pushed the dark, sweat-matted curls off Marsh's forehead. Waited for his languid gaze to focus. "You never told me your name, Cowboy."

Marsh smirked, a new lazy one that Levi thought might be his favorite. Definitely once he heard the answer behind it. "Mr. Levi Bishop."

TWENTY-FIVE

"SOME VIEW." Marsh waited next to a suited Levi, staring out the floor-to-ceiling windows of Eder Capital's corporate headquarters. Vienna looked like a sea of red from the top floor of the city's newest skyscraper, the tile roofs of the shorter surrounding buildings aglow in the afternoon sun.

"My dad used to come home from tours in Europe and tell us about these famous old cities, about the mix of architectural styles. Bella studied it too as part of her engineering degree. Used to show me pictures." Levi adjusted his tie and cuffs. "Seeing it, though, is unreal. It should clash, and it does, but it also works in its own way. Makes you realize how much older these cities are than ours."

Marsh remembered that sense of awe the first time he and Camilla had traveled with Irina to Poland. How small, how unexceptional he'd felt compared to a country and its people who had survived so much more. That feeling had only grown as he'd seen more of the world during his service. "Vienna is centuries older than the oldest

European-founded city in the States. Many of the cities here are. The United States is like the David of countries. A young, surly adolescent who craves attention." He spread his arms wide and see-sawed them. "Moods vary wildly."

Levi's chuckle was cut short by the receptionist descending the internal staircase, her high heels click-clacking on the glass steps. "Ms. Sanders will see you now."

"*Ms.* Sanders?" Sean stood from the reception area chair and buttoned his suit coat. He and Levi had opted for professional attire. So had Marsh, throwing on a blazer with his T-shirt and jeans.

"We had an appointment with Charles Sanders," Sean said.

"*You* had an appointment with Mr. Sanders." She cut a glare at Marsh and Levi. "He's no longer available. But Ms. Sanders has fifteen minutes before her next meeting."

"Well, then," Marsh drawled, detecting her accent was French and figuring his Texas one would grate. "We better hurry up and meet with Ms. Sanders."

If he'd had his phone out, Marsh would've snapped a picture of the woman's narrowed eyes and wrinkled nose and titled it *French Woman Smelling Shit*. He couldn't say he regretted spoiling her day. Levi either, poorly hiding his smile as they followed her up the stairs. His smile died, though, as soon as they stepped into Charles's office.

But not as fast as Marsh's hope went up in flames.

Catherine Sanders stood behind the desk, and if not for his prior knowledge, Marsh might have mistaken her for the woman in the pictures on Levi's mantel back home. Petite, with auburn hair and green eyes, Catherine was a near dead ringer for Levi's late wife. Artificially so. In prior pictures, Catherine's hair had been brown like her brother's. The red was new. Intentional? If so, it had the intended effect. Levi froze midstep, sucked in a harsh breath, and Marsh felt it like a dagger to his heart.

Direct hit, and Catherine knew it, her Cheshire Cat grin wide. "Agents Bishop and Marshall. Mr. Henby-Paxton," she greeted without an extended hand and without offering them a seat. She meant for this to be brief—and unwelcome. "I was surprised to see you on my uncle's schedule today."

Levi came unstuck and shifted, making room for Marsh beside him. Maybe it was the iceberg in her cold, practiced British voice, or maybe it was Marsh's hand on his lower back, but he seemed to come unglued from the past to rejoin them in the present. "We heard your uncle was the man to speak to about tickets to the benefit in Salzburg."

"Surely one of you"—she split a glance between Marsh and Sean—"has the means and the connections."

Marsh removed his hat and claimed a chair, invitation or not. He'd just been punched in the gut; he needed off his feet. "Bureaucracy can be a bitch."

"Don't I know it." She sank into the leather chair behind the desk. "Tell me why you're really here."

An answer was on the tip of Marsh's tongue, but then he spied the chess box on the corner of Charles's desk and a question jumped the line. "Is that a hand-carved Reiter set?" It looked closer to the ones he and Kwan owned from a craftsman with a shop in Stephansplatz. He reached out, picked up the box with its intricate carvings and red inlays, and turned it over.

An edelweiss at the center of the Prater's Ferris wheel carved around the latch.

Standing behind him, Levi sucked in another sharp breath and clasped his shoulder, hard enough to bruise.

"It's a Pincler," Catherine said. "I found his shop when I went wine tasting in Grinzing. My uncle bought that one recently. He's an avid player. I understand you are too, Agent Marshall."

"Marsh," Sean gritted from the chair beside him. "Why don't you put that down?"

He held the box in both hands, judging its weight. It felt right for the box and pieces; nothing extra. While David and Bell hadn't noticed, Marsh had handled more than a few and was familiar with the weight of a board and thirty-two pieces.

He flicked the latch and opened the lid.

Cushioned red velvet and thirty-two pieces.

Levi blew out a held breath.

Catherine's laugh tinkled like church bells off the glass walls. "What were you expecting, Agent Bishop? A bomb?"

"You know something about bombs in chess sets?" Marsh asked.

"No." She crossed one leg over the other and rested her forearms on the desk. "Just going by your husband's reaction. Now, what are you really doing here?"

"We're here about a murder," Marsh said.

"Still? Three years later?" She rapped her manicured nails on the desk. "And isn't that the Federal Police's job?"

Interesting that she'd gone right to Sophie's death when there were more recent murders on the table. And to jurisdiction as her counter.

"You haven't changed your business model the past three years," Sean said.

"No, we haven't. We've actually expanded our philanthropic activities into humanitarian relief for the refugee crisis across Europe."

Marsh scoffed. "That's not the only business you've expanded."

"As I understand it, your friend was in the wrong place at the wrong time."

Levi relaxed his hand on Marsh's shoulder, left it there as he circled to sit on the arm of Marsh's chair. "Coincidences are rare in our line of work."

Catherine twirled a loose lock of hair around her finger, an action so out of character for the corporate image she was projecting—and so in character for the terrorist she was, attempting to emotionally manipulate them. "Is that so, Agent Bishop?"

Levi didn't fall for it. "Your brother was in Amarillo, Texas, recently, checking out a building for purchase. You signed the paperwork to buy it. On behalf of Orchard Investments."

"A client," she said.

"Like Eder Capital is your *client*?"

"Exactly." She heaped on more bullshit. "Stefan was scouting it for me."

"After you purchased it? At the same time we intercepted a trafficking shipment that was supposed to layover there?"

Catherine shifted, and Marsh did not like the interested spark in her eyes. She was enjoying this, matching wits with a new player on the board. "So you're here about a different case? Not about Agent Cohen's murder and not about the benefit? I thought you were suspended, Agent Bishop. I'm sure your superiors would be interested to hear you're here investigating." Her gaze flitted to Sean. "Or your wife's, Mr. Henby-Paxton."

"Like Marsh said," Sean interjected, "we're just here about a murder."

She stood, regarding Sean and him with barely concealed distaste, Levi with disconcerting interest. "And yet you keep missing the obvious, all these years later." She picked up the single folder on the desk and offered it to Levi. "Your invitations will be delivered to the embassy. Mr. Henby-Paxton, we'll expect Paxton Industries to make a matching grant."

"Not to your *client*'s organization," Sean retorted.

"To the charity of your choice," she finished. "You can speak to my uncle and brother at the benefit."

Levi waited for her to leave, for Sean to swing the glass door shut behind her, before opening the folder.

To a stack of photos of Sophie and Stefan, in one compromising situation after another. The last picture the most damning of all. The two of them stood together in a cinch outside the Karlsplatz U-Bahn station, snow falling at the entrance where he and Levi had stood on Friday, Sophie in a long winter trench, the ends of her coat caught by the wind, exposing the red chiffon of a long red ball gown underneath.

Levi spoke the terrible truth staring them in the face. "That's the night she was murdered."

TWENTY-SIX

FOR AS GOOD a shape as Levi was in, those couple of inches Marsh had on him were turning the brisk walk to Wagner's place into a sprint for him. Adjacent to the city center, Sean had called this district Josefstadt when he'd suggested they take a car or the U-Bahn. Marsh had ignored him and hoofed it on foot. By the time they were in the elevator of a modern, oddly shaped building across from a park and Gothic cathedral, Levi was a sweaty mess from the tips of his hair to the valleys between his toes. "Maybe we shouldn't do this at his house." Levi yanked loose his tie and shucked out of his jacket. "Why don't we set up a meeting somewhere else? Give you some time to cool down?"

The elevator doors opened, and Marsh led the march down the hallway. "Those photo stills were from local police surveillance. I know where all the cameras were that night. That angle, that camera, it was Wagner's. And we were blacked out that day."

"Because our government didn't pay its bills," Sean said.

Marsh rounded on Sean. "Do you honestly believe he didn't know?" He jutted his chin at the folder in Sean's hand. "That he didn't see those photos or know about Sophie and Stefan? Someone kept those from us."

The door at the end of the hall swung open, and an impeccably styled man filled the condo doorway. Middle-aged, he was shorter than Levi and as broad as Marsh, a solid wall of muscle in designer athletic threads, his expression like thunder, blue eyes hard and shooting daggers at Marsh. "Well, this explains my husband's shitty mood."

"Philippe."

Wagner's husband ran a shaky hand over his spiky blond hair. "I had hoped you were gone for good, but no such luck."

"We need to speak to Teddy," Sean cut in. "Dispatch said he called in sick today."

"Because he came home at two in the morning," he answered snidely, then shifted his icy glare back to Marsh. "Did you have anything to do with that?"

"Let them in, Phil," Wagner called from somewhere in the apartment.

Philippe's body didn't move, but his gaze landed on Levi for the first time. "I don't know you." His diction was perfect despite the simmering anger, his British accent the opposite of Wagner's, high class and proper, similar to Catherine's but less practiced, more like Levi was used to hearing in those Merchant Ivory films Kristin used to love.

Levi didn't bother extending his hand, figuring it would be unwelcome. "Special Agent Levi Bishop, Agent Marshall's husband."

Eyes wide, Philippe spun on his heel and charged inside, facing down Wagner in the middle of the living area. "That's why you've been on a bender all weekend?"

"Not now, Phil." He winced, acting and looking like he'd just rolled out of bed, shirtless and in sweats, his blond waves tousled and jaw covered in dark stubble.

"When, Teddy? Or are you going to pine forever? You married me. Me, Teddy!" He shoved Wagner's chest with both hands. "A decade before he ever showed up in his stupid fucking hat and boots." Shoved him again, out of the way so he could storm deeper into the condo, a door somewhere slamming in his wake.

"Where can we talk?" Marsh said.

"The listening room." Wagner led them the opposite direction from where Philippe had disappeared, through the living area, past the kitchen and dining area, and down a long hallway to one of the rooms at the end. By the time they reached their destination, Levi had mentally calculated six figures' worth of furnishings and knickknacks and added another six figures in audio gear inside the room.

"Let me go grab a shirt," Wagner said, leaving the three of them alone in the room.

Marsh tucked into the corner of the chaise, and Sean sank into one of the club chairs while Levi examined the wall of audio components he could only dream of owning one day in the forever distant future. "Philippe's an interior designer, correct?"

Sean nodded. "Has his own firm."

Even with his own firm, even with designer discounts, something wasn't adding up. Levi withdrew his phone and shot off an email to Holt, hoping it wasn't too early on the

West Coast, hoping to get an answer before they were ready to leave here.

Wagner materialized in jeans and a tee, face damp and hair combed back, looking more alert if still hungover. "You should have called before showing up here."

"Would you have answered?" Marsh replied.

Ignoring him, Wagner met Levi in the middle of the room, hand extended. "I should have known he'd married the hottest guy at the bar. Teddy Wagner."

"Levi Bishop."

"Congratulations. I'd toast you too, but I think I've had enough booze to last me the rest of the year." Wagner was charming in that rough-around-the-edges, hot-guy-next-door sort of way. Someone you'd want to grab a drink with. But how much was he hiding behind that everyman exterior?

Marsh wasn't waiting to find out, going straight for the jugular. "Sophie was having an affair with Stefan Sanders. You knew." Not a question, a statement.

A truth Wagner acknowledged as he sank into the other club chair, propped his elbows on his knees, and hung his head, raking his hands through his hair. "Who told you?"

"Catherine Sanders," Sean answered.

He whipped his gaze back up. "She knows?"

"That's not the point," Marsh snapped. "Why don't we? Does Binny?"

"No. Not that I know of." He dropped his arms and left them hanging over his knees. "She asked me to keep it from him. And from you two."

"Why?"

"She said it was an op. That you would never go for it."

"Was it just an op?" Levi asked as he lowered himself onto the chaise beside Marsh.

"I don't think so." Wagner rose, crossed the room to the acoustic panel on the far wall, and swung it open, exposing a wall safe behind it. From inside it, he withdrew a laptop and flash drive and brought them back to the coffee table. He booted up the computer, inserted the drive, and opened one of the unmarked folders. The screen filled with pictures, all of them Sophie and Stefan, all looking as real as the ones Catherine had shown them. Some more so, hand-held selfies and close-up photos.

"Why were we blacked out the day of the bombing?" Marsh asked.

"That was your government's doing. Not mine."

"Stewart Anthony," Levi suggested. "He was one of the congresspeople holding up budget approval, a rather vocal opponent if I recall correctly."

"Why didn't you show us these, Wags?" Marsh said, some of the fire gone out of his voice, the sting of betrayal filling its place. "After the bombing?"

"Because I was ordered not to."

"By whom?"

"My boss, the superintendent for Vienna."

Marsh and Sean lurched forward, the latter asking, "Why didn't you tell us that?"

"Because despite the fact we cooperated"—he gestured among the three of them—"I don't work for you or your country. There is a chain of command here in Vienna and at the Federal Police that I am obliged to obey. And you two fucking left." Betrayal colored his voice too, cutting off any other words for several long seconds.

Levi wanted to say something, to ask all the follow-up

questions filling his head, but there was more involved here than his own investigative curiosity. Wagner had been Marsh's and Sean's friend and colleague, he'd been put in a no-win situation, same as Marsh and Sean, and the three of them had to come to terms with that if their present investigation was to move forward. Because they couldn't chase Stefan Sanders on their own here; they needed Wagner and the Federal Police. But was the will there to do it? "Where'd the internal investigation go?" Marsh asked Wagner, arriving at the same question.

"Fucking nowhere." He shut the laptop, yanked out the flash drive, and slapped it into Marsh's palm. "I've been conducting my own with the tools you gave me. Everything I've found is on there. But I still can't conclusively tie the bombing to Eder. Maybe a thread you have will."

"Thank you." Marsh closed his fingers around the flash drive. "Did you talk to Ross about any of this?"

Wagner shook his head. "Sophie didn't trust him."

Another strike in the Ross column. But Levi was still curious about the ones in Wagner's. "Teddy, how do you afford this place on an inspector's salary?"

"Philippe takes care of the house out of his."

"Do you have any idea how much some of this costs?"

"I don't care." He waved a dismissive hand. "I could live in a tent in the woods and be fine. I did. I'd rather—"

"You'd rather what?" Marsh said.

Wagner averted his gaze. "It doesn't matter."

"Are you torn up because of me or because of this?" He gestured at the laptop, at the flash drive in his hand.

"I hated lying to you." His voice cracked, years of recriminations bubbling to the surface. "I knew what she meant to you. Maybe if I'd told you…" He covered his face with his hands and choked back a sob.

Marsh rose to go to him but stopped short when Philippe appeared in the doorway. "That's enough. You can leave now." He sat on the arm of Wagner's chair and draped an arm around his husband's shoulders. "I'll take care of him."

Wagner curled into Philippe, hiding his face against his leg, Philippe's fingers carding through his hair, a kiss, and an "I'll be right back, love," before standing to see them out. Sean spoke quietly to him, giving their regards and asking that Philippe keep them updated. Marsh was silent, fist clenched around the flash drive. Levi pulled up the rear, checking his phone.

Reading the timely reply from Holt.

He paused just outside the doorway, a last-minute question for the designer, a follow-up that had to be asked. "You do a lot of work for Calex Enterprises?"

Philippe nodded. "They have properties in Vienna, London, and several cities in the States, commercial and residential. Keeps me busy."

"Who's your contact at Calex?"

He tightened his grip on the door, knuckles white. "I don't have to tell you that."

"Is it Catherine Sanders?"

He slammed the door in Levi's face.

TWENTY-SEVEN

MARSH EXITED WAGNER'S BUILDING, inhaled the soupy summer air, and made no objection to Sean's suggestion they take the U-Bahn back to the penthouse. The hair under his Stetson was wet from the earlier sprint, and Levi's dress shirt wasn't faring much better. He had no idea how Sean was still in his jacket and tie.

There was no need to press themselves to melting any longer; hadn't really been in the first place. They'd hit another brick wall. Or rather Wagner had. Marsh was still angry Wagner had kept the truth from him, but he could commiserate, having been stymied himself for years. He'd likewise been manipulated from on high and prevented from doing his job. He also hated that his friend's life, professionally and personally, was a train wreck. Hated that he in any way had contributed to the breakdown. Marsh didn't see how to help the personal situation—that was between Wags and Philippe—but maybe the flash drive in his pocket could help professionally.

Or maybe Levi's final curveball question would.

"What was that about Calex?" Marsh asked as they emerged from the station a couple blocks from Sean's building.

"Their flat reminded me of Aunt Liz's place. I'd seen some of those items, some of that furniture, or items like it before. High-end shit. It didn't make sense on a cop's salary, and interior designers do well and get discounts, but few, I imagine, do that well or get discounts enough to pay for that place and everything inside it."

"Holt was already digging into Philippe's financials," Sean said as they wove through people and construction barrels, accessibility improvements in progress across the city.

"I texted and asked him to book it. He turned up Calex, which while not directly tied to Eder or Catherine Sanders, used the same attorney as Eder and Orchard to file their foreign business papers in the US and is headquartered in, take a wild guess…"

Not too hard to make that one. Marsh wouldn't even call it wild. "Vienna."

Levi made a keep going gesture with his hand and flicked his gaze toward the downtown skyscrapers. "Getting warmer."

"In the same building as Eder Capital?"

"Bingo!" Levi said with an Oprah-worthy, you-get-a-car flourish, nearly knocking over a barrel.

Sean was more circumspect. "She could be paying him for design—"

The squeal of tires and the alarmed shouts of pedestrians cut short Sean's words. Marsh whipped his gaze the direction of the commotion. A black Mercedes sedan barreled through the crosswalk a block away, speeding the direction of the crosswalk the three of them had just stepped into with a herd of other people.

"Everyone out of the road!" Levi shouted as the three of them kicked into action, even Sean who'd been out of law enforcement for a year. Sean and Levi surged forward, the former shouting, "Bewegen! Bewegen!" as they hurried half the crowd to the opposite curb. Marsh spun, arms wide, and shouted "Polizei! Komm zurück!" forcing his half of the crowd back onto the curb they'd just stepped off, several staggering as they crashed into the construction barrels, but at least they were out of the road.

All except one. "Mama!" A little girl about Lily's age raced into the road, separated from her mother in the commotion. Marsh did the split-second calculations. There was no way she'd make it to the other side before the charging Mercedes plowed through the crosswalk. Even less chance when she stumbled, and the Benz failed to brake.

Levi made the same calculations, locked eyes with Marsh, and sprinted into the intersection. Marsh stepped off the curb, prepared to put himself between the charging car and Levi and the girl. From the opposite curb, Sean, who had his arms wrapped around a screaming woman, the child's mother no doubt, shouted, "The barrels, Marsh! Grab a barrel."

A risk, the car could swerve, hit the other pedestrians, but the only chance at saving the ones in the middle of the crosswalk. Marsh spied the nearest barrel a pedestrian had already knocked over and yanked it off its mooring. "Everybody get back!" he yelled in German, Sean doing the same on the other side of the road. He lifted the barrel over his head and heaved it into the oncoming path of the vehicle. The Benz swerved, narrowly skating between where Levi was using his body to shield the child and the curb. Marsh heaved a relieved sigh and thanked his saints.

Only to curse when the chaos magnified tenfold. Shots rang out from above them, from one of the upstairs windows over the ground-floor restaurant, and Levi hit the deck, covering the girl. Sean and Marsh revised their directives, shouting "Get down!" and moving people back to the cover of the buildings.

But Levi was out there in the middle of the street, exposed.

Another round of shots rang out, stalling Marsh's sprint into the street, forcing him down. Forcing him to reassess the shooter's target. It wasn't Levi, or him, or Sean.

It was the car.

A third flurry of shots, one hitting the Benz's back right tire and causing it to spin. Enough for Marsh to glimpse the driver. Buzzed brown hair, broken nose, thick neck, tattoos.

Stefan Sanders.

The facilitator, the attempted murderer, wrenched the wheel, righted the car, and hit the gas. With run flats for tires, he could make it another few miles before he had to ditch the car. They weren't likely to catch Stefan… but they could catch their other suspect at the scene.

Levi made the same assessment. Crouched, he carried the child to the curb, handed her to her sobbing mother, then sprinted toward the building. "I'm going after the shooter."

Marsh took off after Levi. "Stairs?" Levi asked the restaurant hostess watching from the front door, but something down the side alley caught Marsh's eye.

"Bishop! Around back!" He hustled into the narrow,

shadowed alley, no footsteps behind him but a small figure running flat out in front of him. "Halt!" he shouted to no avail, the figure disappearing around a corner.

And reaching a dead end.

A young woman, white, her clothes too big, her long dark hair stringy and matted, clutched the chain-link fence with one hand, a knife in the other. Crying, she mumbled "I'm sorry" in German, over and over again.

"It's okay." Marsh spoke in German as he slowly approached behind her. "Why don't you put down the knife, and we can talk about it."

She spun and fell back against the fence. "I just want it to be over."

Marsh took a step forward. "Want what to be over?"

"All of it," she said in English, and raised the knife to her throat.

Took another step. "What's your name, sweetheart?"

"Maria." She closed her eyes and shook her head, the chain-link fence rattling.

Levi appeared at the back screen door of the restaurant, poised to move.

Eyes still closed, Maria's voice, her entire being was full of defeat. "I just need it to be over." Heartbreaking, the intention final.

Marsh nodded, and Levi slammed open the screen door. Maria's eyes popped open, her gaze following the sudden sound, and Marsh lunged forward, knocking loose the knife. A split second before Levi launched himself from the top step, wrapped his arms around Maria, and took her down in an academy-perfect roll.

Suspect secure.

TWENTY-EIGHT

MARSH WOULD HAVE PREFERRED to take Maria to the US Embassy for questioning. Someone with the Federal Police was aiding and abetting Eder's criminal empire. Ross could be too, but that was less certain. But with the crowd of bystanders, the number of emergency calls received, and the amount of video footage already on the internet, there was no escaping the Federal Police taking charge of the incident.

Their saving grace had been Wagner's appearance at the scene. He looked markedly better than he had at his condo, calm and in control, which was enough to convince the officer in charge that the incident was related to a joint task force that Wagner oversaw for the police. A defunct task force including a retired agent and two suspended ones, but thankfully the officer didn't check too closely, more than happy to turn the scene over. But they would only get so far, so long, before their lie was discovered. Which was why they needed to interrogate their suspect sooner rather than later before someone pulled a Bell and yanked them off the investigation.

Wagner exited the interrogation room and joined Marsh, Levi, Sean, and Ross on the crowded observation side of the glass. Marsh had called the latter down to the station, despite Sophie's doubts and despite Levi also asking if it was the best idea. Maybe it wasn't, but it was also a test. Marsh wanted to see what, if anything, got back to Eder Capital or Catherine Sanders.

"Did you get a last name?" Levi asked. They'd been held up giving their own statements and had arrived after Wagner had already asked the record basics.

Wagner's expression was grim; they weren't going to like the answer. "Bauer."

Marsh staggered, catching himself on the observation desk. "Bauer? As in Peter Bauer? The same Peter Bauer who walked into Karlsplatz station with a bomb under his trench coat and killed Sophie and nine others?"

"Yes, she's that Peter Bauer's sister."

Sean ran a hand down his tired face, and Ross, forearms braced on the chair back, hung his head. "Whose fucking payroll are these people on?"

Levi, the only one who didn't look like he'd been punched in the gut, asked, "How's her English?"

"Seems fluent," Wagner answered.

"Let me take a run at her," he proposed. "I'm a new face with a new angle."

"You're suspended," Ross said, straightening. "You're not even supposed to be here much less in the room with her."

"And none of you"—Wagner swung a stern glare around the room—"have jurisdiction." The same argument

Catherine had used. Also the same argument any cop with half a brain would use.

"So come into the room with me," Levi countered. He split a glance between Ross and Wagner. "Both of you if you need to."

Wagner's indigo eyes flicked Marsh's direction. "You okay with that?"

"Don't ask me. He doesn't need my permission. He's my partner on this case."

"No offense meant," Wagner replied with a raised hand, then headed for the door. "Let me go get my file on Bauer. We should have forensics back by now too."

"Get a picture of Stefan too, please."

While they waited for him to return, Sean asked Levi, "What new angle?" That part of Levi's proposal had intrigued Marsh too.

"Let me play it out."

Good enough for Marsh and for Sean. Ross looked skeptical but followed their lead. Marsh for one couldn't wait to watch Levi work. Wagner reentered with two file folders. Levi flipped through them, brow wrinkled in concentration. But he was nodding; good material, then. "This'll work. Thank you," he told Wagner as he snapped shut the folders. "Let's do this."

Marsh held the door open for the group, then after closing it behind them, leaned a shoulder against the wall by the observation glass. On the other side, Wagner reclaimed his chair across from Maria, but Levi didn't take the one beside him. He rounded the table and pulled out the chair next to Maria instead. Sinking into it, he braced his forearms on his knees, the two folders dangling from his fingertips.

"He's good," Sean said from his spot at the desk. "Below her eye level, giving her the perception of power and congeniality."

Marsh smirked. "I know."

"Maria, I'm Special Agent Levi Bishop with the FBI. I'm sorry I didn't get to introduce myself earlier. Are you okay if we chat in English?"

She nodded and shifted toward Levi in her metal chair. She probably didn't even realize it, but any trained interrogator would. Levi was connecting with her, winning her trust. "You've already met Chief Inspector Wagner," he said. "That's Special Agent Ross over there brooding against the wall. He works for the FBI too here in Vienna."

She briefly looked them over, then brought her gaze back to Levi. Good. He had her attention, and her trust, more than anyone else in the room. He withdrew a photo from the thinner of the two folders and held it out to her, forcing her to take it instead of setting it on the table in front of her. "We found this weapon abandoned in the building near where the shots were fired from today. Your prints are on the weapon." He handed her another photo. "You're also on camera leaving the side door of the building." He passed her a third. "Before we stopped you from using this to kill yourself." The knife then, to which she closed her eyes and looked away, swallowing hard.

With her eyes still closed, she didn't see Levi riffle through the much thicker file. Didn't see the picture he did place on the table. "This is your brother, Peter." Her eyes flew open, going straight to the photo. "He died three years ago on a similar mission." Then darted up to Levi. "Am I right? You were both sent to kill someone?"

"I don't know what you're talking about," she said.

He laid Stefan Sanders's picture on top of Peter's. "Was this your target?"

Maria didn't reply, but her eyes became glassy, wetness gathering at the corners.

"Was he your brother's target too?" Levi said, and Marsh understood his new angle, where this was going. To an alternate theory of the events of that night three years ago. One that the rest of them had been too close to the event to see. A more objective observer, Levi had seen the larger forest and found a place for those photos of Stefan and Sophie.

"I just want this to be over." A repeat of what she'd said when they'd cornered her in the alley. But then she said more. "I just want my family to be free."

"Free?" Wagner said. "You're Austrian citizens."

She swallowed hard. "My parents were missionaries in Kosovo. They were so busy." She reached out and moved the picture of Stefan so she could see the one of her brother again. Lightly, lovingly, she laid her fingertips on his cheek. "They didn't notice Peter slipping away. He got addicted to drugs, indebted to bad people there." The ISIS cell they'd tied him to. She drew back her hand. "When we got home, he got clean. I thought we were free. But the bad people were here too. And so was she."

"Catherine Sanders," Levi said.

Maria nodded. "She told Peter she could wipe out his debt, could make the terrorists and dealers go away, and we would all be free if he just did this one thing."

"Kill her brother." Wagner offered her a box of tissues. He wasn't too bad an interrogator himself.

Maria snagged several. "She left us alone after Peter died. I thought we were free, but then I saw her and her brother at an event later that year. I knew we never would be. Not really."

"She came back to collect," Wagner suggested.

"Three days ago," Maria replied. "Said it was my turn. Said if I didn't do what she told me, she would have my entire family wiped out."

"What did she tell you to do, Maria?" Levi asked.

Marsh leaned forward, anticipating the awful answer. "To answer the call when she rang. And she did. Today. She told me when and where Stefan would be and said a rifle would be waiting."

"She told you to kill him?"

"Yes."

TWENTY-NINE

IT WAS the next morning before they reconvened due to the clusterfuck the previous day had devolved into. Especially for Wagner. He'd had to finish booking Maria, interview witnesses, process incoming forensics, and coordinate the search for the driver of the black Benz that was found abandoned several miles from the scene. Levi, like Marsh and Sean, had identified Stefan Sanders as the driver, and while Wagner believed them, while Maria had confessed to being there for the express purpose of killing Stefan Sanders, the fact that travel records still showed him in the US was a hurdle.

Ross didn't have much better of a yesterday, dealing with the mess Levi, Marsh, and Sean had created by pretending to be cops at the scene. Levi agreed that it had been the right call at the time, the quickest way to move potential victims out of the way of the speeding vehicle, but Wagner's boss, the one who'd shut down his investigation, was coming down on them hard, threatening a diplomatic shitstorm. Eventually, Ross had told them to get the hell out of the station so he could try to smooth things over.

Which was how they all ended up at the US embassy the next morning, Marsh, Levi, and Sean making official statements that their actions yesterday had been for the sole purpose of saving innocent lives. They formally apologized for the overstep and hoped it was enough to put out that particular fire.

While they stoked another. Levi admired his husband at the head of the conference table, the fact that Marsh couldn't not take charge to save his life. It chafed sometimes, but it was also sexy as hell. "All right," Marsh said. "Theories. Go."

"Catherine wants Stefan gone," Wagner said. "Because he's the heir."

"Or because he was fucking Sophie," Ross countered. "A traitor." They'd filled him in on that fact, a revelation that had resulted in Ross storming into his office, slamming his door, and throwing things. After that, Levi was fairly convinced Ross was not Eder Capital's mole inside the FBI. He'd been as surprised as them by the Sophie-Stefan news. And angry as hell—at Sophie, at Wagner, at Binny, who Levi was fairly convinced knew more than he was letting on to anyone, possibly even to Ajay.

"Catherine's had Stefan in line for three years," Sean said. "What's changed?"

"We're back and closing in," Marsh posited. "If we believe what Sophie told Wags, Stefan was an op." Ross scoffed—Levi mentally agreed—but Marsh kept going, undeterred. "She had something on him, and when she died, he was out from under her thumb. Now we're back, and if we find out what Sophie had, we can use it against him too. So what did Sophie know?"

"Maybe he was just in love with her," Wagner said. "He's covering up his mistakes."

"And Catherine is done with him altogether," Ross added.

Marsh shook his head. "That can't be all there *was*. That can't be all there *is*."

"We need to see Sophie's files," Levi said. "All of them."

"I thought I had everything," Marsh replied.

"And we're back to Binny," Sean said. "Keeping something from us."

"Fuck." Marsh spun from the table, hands laced behind his head, pacing. Levi reached out and laid a hand on his arm as he passed, creating a connection while a different one was unraveling.

Marsh squeezed his hand, link acknowledged, then continued pacing. "This is a bad bishop nightmare."

"A what?" Levi asked. "I assume that refers to a chess term and not me."

Marsh's chuckle was a welcome one, a release of tension. "A bad bishop is one that's cornered behind its own pawns. No good way out."

Levi didn't believe that. There had to be a way through this.

Through it.

Through the Sanders family and the brewing internal conflict Levi and his team could manipulate to bring the entire Eder Capital operation down. "Do you think Charles knows what's going on between his niblings?"

Marsh caught on, albeit from a slightly different angle.

"There was a falling out between their parents and Charles. Maybe the parents can shed some light on things." He looked across the table at Wagner. "Are they staying in Vienna?"

"Salzburg."

"What if this is vengeance?"

"Whose?" Sean asked.

"Stefan or Catherine, on behalf of their parents."

"And the other is still Team Charles," Ross said, playing it out. "But which one? And vengeance for what?"

On that note, Levi circled back to where they'd begun, tying it all together. "What if there's leverage of some sort over the parents, and Sophie promised to get them clear if Stefan delivered evidence of the trafficking?"

"I like where this is headed," Marsh said. "But why would Stefan try to kill us? Why not try to work the same deal with us as he did with Sophie?

"Because he's made that deal with Catherine already."

"Why would she?" Wagner asked. "The woman's ice cold. I don't think it's because she cares for them."

"Stefan must have something she needs," Marsh said.

"But she doesn't trust he won't turn traitor again," Ross added. "Thinks she could get it herself."

Levi propped his elbows on the table and scrubbed his hands over his face, wanting to scream but holding it in. Barely. "Something doesn't add up, and we're pretzeling ourselves to figure it out. We're getting lost in the weeds."

"Which, if Binny is the mole"—Sean held up both hands, palms out, a don't-shoot-the-messenger gesture— "lost in the weeds is exactly where he wants us. Why he gave Marsh those files in the first place. To send us down this rabbit hole."

Marsh stopped at the head of the table and braced his

hands on the edge, looking as frustrated as Levi felt. "Okay, big picture, how do we take these assholes down? What threads do we have still to pull that can help unravel this knot?"

"Pretzel," Levi mumbled, aiming to poke a hole in the rising tension. It worked, laughter rumbling around the table, including from Marsh at the head.

"Pretzel," he conceded. "Now I fucking want one, so let's wrap this up."

"The parents," Ross said, answering Marsh's question. "I have initial background searches in our files. No red flags. Wags, can you help me dig deeper?"

Wagner nodded. "I'll also make a list of colleagues I suspect are on Eder's payroll, starting with my boss, though I think it goes higher. I'll also talk to Philippe about Calex. I doubt he understands what he's involved in. I should be the one to tell him."

Levi appreciated his willingness to go there. Watched in admiration as Marsh squeezed his friend's shoulder, offering support. Waited until their moment passed before tossing out another lead. "The chess boxes," he said. "Here and stateside."

"We'll go check out Pincler's shop in Grinzing," Marsh said.

"And I'll also follow up with Holt and the team in San Diego," Levi added. "On the boxes delivered there and on the shelter's debt Catherine tried to leverage."

"I'll touch base with Charlie," Sean said. "Find out if Anthony or anyone in the Bureau has tried to interfere again, including Binny."

Marsh nodded, all to his liking it seemed. "Big picture, we need to know who is standing behind the pawns. We gather the evidence we need and turn the pawns we can to reach them. That's how we end this. That's how we shut Eder Capital down."

They all rose, prepared to get started on their to-do lists, when the conference room door opened, Ross's assistant poking her head in. "Agents, these just arrived for you." She handed Ross a stack of stark white envelopes.

"Your invitations," Ross said, handing one each to Levi, Marsh, and Sean.

Levi judged the weight of his, heavy, expensive card-stock, his name and title written on the front in calligraphy. He slid his index finger under the lip to pop it open. The embossed card inside invited him to the Eder Capital Relief for Refugee Benefit Gala at the Sanders Family Estate in Salzburg that weekend.

"Well," Marsh drawled, "I guess we're in."

Levi went to tuck his invite back into the envelope—and met resistance. Setting the invite on the table, he squeezed either end of the envelope, opening it more. There was a folded strip of paper at the bottom. "There's something else in mine." He drew out the note, Marsh peering over his shoulder, his hand on Levi's hip, as Levi read it aloud.

Karlsplatz Station Square. Wednesday. 10 a.m. Come alone. —Catherine

Marsh dug his fingers into his hip hard enough to bruise.

THIRTY

MARSH LEANED against the side of the SUV parked a block away from Karlsplatz and considered his husband. "Are you sure you want to do this?"

Marsh was sure he did not want Levi to do this, but it wasn't his call. Back in Amarillo, he'd sworn to himself to not stand in Levi's way when it came to doing his job. His husband was a smart, competent agent with sharp instincts. But that was the professional side of the equation. Personally, Levi was his husband and about to go toe to toe with a murderer, a woman who had twice tried to kill her own brother.

Levi, however, was fearless, all business this morning as he rolled up his shirt sleeves and prepared to do battle. "I'm sure I want to get to the bottom of this and get home. I miss my son."

Marsh missed David too, but he'd also promised David he would keep Levi safe and bring him back home. He wouldn't break that promise. "We might not be able to hear you down there. She might force you onto a train. Someone at the Federal Police may get wind of this meet and cut the station surveillance feeds. If I can't—"

Levi silenced him with a kiss and pinned him against the SUV while he argued his case with his tongue and lips. Marsh gripped the front of his shirt, never wanting to let him go yet knowing he had to because Levi was right. This was business. Marsh needed to trust Levi to do his job. Let that trust quell the personal fear inherent in the situation. He uncurled his fingers and smoothed out the wrinkles he'd created.

Levi lifted his face with a finger under his chin. "Nothing I said before we left Texas has changed. I will come back to you. I will give you a home with me and David."

"You can't be cer—"

Levi's second kiss was brief and to the point, a period on the argument. "With you at my side, I am." He didn't give Marsh a chance to counter further. He turned and strode the length of the block to the station entrance and disappeared into the tunnel's shadow.

Marsh hauled ass into the SUV. Grabbing his tablet from beside the seat, he propped it open on the dash and laid his keyboard across his lap.

"You love him, don't you?" Sean said from the driver's seat beside him.

"Not gonna tell you before I say it to him." But yes, Marsh had been falling for his husband since he'd first laid eyes on him, harder as he got to know the amazing father, son, brother, agent, and partner he was. And after being back here in Vienna, in the trappings of his old life, he was more certain than ever that he wanted the new one with Levi and David. Yes, that four letter word was grafting itself onto his bones, flowing in the blood that raced through his heart, deeper and stronger with each argument Levi made. Convincing Marsh a little each day that those three terrifying words wouldn't break him if he said them to Levi.

Sean just smiled and patted his shoulder. "I'm happy for you."

Marsh rolled his eyes and tucked the comm into his ear. "I'll be happy when my husband walks back out of that station alive."

"I'll walk out of here alive," Levi replied. "Copy that?"

Marsh chuckled. "Copy."

Levi continued to report his location as he navigated the station, Marsh hopping camera to camera with him. No issues with reception or feeds, including when Levi rode the escalator down to the Red Line platform. Marsh spotted Catherine before Levi did, sitting on the farthest bench from the escalators, nearest the tunnel.

"That's a good sign," Sean said. "She's not looking to make a spectacle."

"She could be looking to throw him in front of the train."

"My husband, ever the pessimist," Levi said in a dry, droll tone. "I've got this."

His confident voice, his equally confident strut, said he did. So too did his expression. The confidence turned Marsh on. The flirtatious glint in his blue eyes turned his stomach, the expression, the heat, too similar to the expression he'd worn for Marsh the other night when they'd role-played strangers in a bar.

Catherine lifted her bag to make room for him on the bench. "I wasn't sure you'd come."

"You delivered the invitations we asked for. Seemed the least I could do." He sat and crossed his legs her direction. Marsh barely stopped his hands from clenching. He worked the keyboard instead, zooming the camera in, watching for any tells that might compromise Levi. He saw none. "And I had some questions."

"Such as?"

"Why are you trying to kill your brother?"

Catherine laughed, that same tinkling sound from the office the other day. She was evil, yet her laugh sounded like what Marsh thought an angel's must. "A straight shooter just like your husband."

"Not exactly straight," Levi said with a wink.

Her laughter subsided into a wide, easy smile. It was no wonder she'd fooled so many people into thinking she was just an investment banker who worked for the family business on the side. "I can see why Agent Marshall likes you. You like him?"

"I married him."

"Oh, now that's an interesting answer." She angled his direction, wrists resting atop her crossed knees. "Not exactly to the question I asked, Agent Bishop."

He parried with a teasing smile. "You didn't answer my question either, Ms. Sanders."

The loudspeaker announced the approaching train.

Catherine didn't bother to speak louder, and with the increasing background noise, Marsh had to strain to hear. "I didn't try to kill my brother. Maria Bauer did."

"After he tried to kill us."

She wrinkled her nose. "I don't think Stefan likes you very much."

"And you do?"

"I sent you that invitation, didn't I?" She stood as the train pulled into the station, grabbed her bag, and beckoned Levi to follow. "Ride with me."

Levi didn't hesitate. He stood in the subway car's open doorway, gesturing politely for her to enter first.

Marsh wished like hell he'd said those three terrifying words. In the minutes of audio static that followed, he wished like hell he'd said a lot of things to Levi that had been on the tip of his tongue for weeks. Wished like hell, professional boundaries be damned, that he'd never let Levi go down into that station alone, that he'd never agreed to the meet with Catherine, that he'd convinced Levi to stay in Texas.

Wondered in the back of his mind if he should have ever involved Levi in the first place, if he'd compromised a good man, a good father, by putting him on the radar of a viper who would do anything to get what she wanted.

Sean gently clasped his biceps. "Breathe, Marsh."

Marsh slammed shut his eyes. He couldn't watch the empty station, see the empty platform where his husband was a moment ago. He'd lost him, had broken his promise to David, wouldn't be able to bring his father back home to him, safe and—

"Taubstummengasse," Levi said in his butchered German. "We're only one station down."

Marsh opened his eyes, sucked in air, then struck keys like his life depended on it, accessing the surveillance feeds for the new station.

"There!" Sean pointed at the top left corner of the tablet screen.

Marsh redirected the nearest camera, zoomed in, and wanted to hurl. Catherine and Levi were walking arm in arm, Levi's flirtatious smile turned up to ten. "Surely, we could have walked?"

"I have a class at the Diplomatic Academy in five," Catherine replied. "This was quicker, and you'll get a chance to look around. It's a lovely building."

"A class? You teach?"

"The intersection of corporate philanthropy and diplomatic policy."

Levi laughed out loud. "That's rich."

She stopped just shy of the entrance, still in shadow but with the sun threatening her toes. She leaned closer and lowered her voice. "Not as rich as two FBI agents marrying to skirt one getting thrown off a case and the other's debts."

Marsh froze.

Levi shrugged. Fucking shrugged. "We do what we have to do."

"Is that what you're still doing? What you have to?"

"That's what I'll always do to protect the ones I love."

Catherine's evil satisfied smile would win her a one-way ticket to hell. "That's good to hear, Agent Bishop."

Marsh tossed his keyboard and earpiece to the floorboard, staggered out of the SUV, and puked.

THIRTY-ONE

SEAN HAD WARNED HIM. **Meet us at the pub. Marsh did not handle that well**, his text had read. Levi had worried about that. Marsh had been on edge about the whole meet, and the second Levi had stepped onto that train, Marsh had no doubt gone over the edge into the abyss.

Sean's warning, Levi's worry, didn't do the reality Levi walked into justice. He stood near the pub's entrance, watching as his husband polished off a second stein of beer, and it wasn't even noon yet. Marsh slammed the glass onto the table, next to the other empty, and looked up for the server. And saw Levi instead.

Oh.

The day drinking wasn't the worst of it. Marsh looked wrecked and not in the good way. His hair was a mess like he'd run his hands through it countless times, his shoulders were tight, his jaw was clenched, and his eyes… Levi had never wanted to see that look directed at him. Anger, doubt, and fear, the last hitting Levi like a tsunami.

Fuck.

He crossed the pub to the U-shaped booth Marsh occupied. Levi slid into the end across from him, Sean between them at the back of the booth. His ass had barely hit the wood seat when Marsh began his interrogation. "What else did she say to you between stations?"

"Nothing."

"Nothing?" He scoffed. "You walked off that train, arm in arm, and you expect us to believe nothing else was said."

"Yes." As much as the accusatory words and tone rankled, Levi understood where Marsh's anger was coming from and tried not to take it personally. "Have I given you any reason to think I'd lie to you?"

Marsh pressed his lips together. Good. His brain knew the correct answer, even if his heart was shouting otherwise.

Levi continued. "I started to speak, to ask Catherine whether Stefan would still be at the benefit, and she said she couldn't hear, so I didn't say anything else until after we got off the train."

"She's looking for a way in," Sean said.

"That was obvious. Hopefully, I fooled her into thinking she has one."

Marsh shifted forward, forearms resting on the table. "Fooled her?"

"I sold it. We've had enough practice the past month." Marsh jerked back like he'd been slapped, and Levi immediately regretted his choice of words. "Marsh, fuck, I didn't mean—"

He bolted out of the booth faster than any man his size should be able to move. "I'm going to the bathroom."

Levi moved almost as fast, only a step behind as Marsh

ducked into the narrow back hallway. Near the end, when it looked like he was about to turn into the bathroom, Levi called out, "Keep walking." Marsh obeyed, slamming out the back door with both hands, but then he kept walking like he was going to walk right out of the alley and away from him. "Marsh, stop!"

He halted but didn't turn around, his back to Levi, his hands fisted at his sides.

Levi reserved several feet of the distance between them, sensing Marsh needed those couple of seconds to cool down. "We set ground rules when we started this. Do you remember what those were?"

Marsh flung back his head and laughed, the bitter sound bouncing off stone walls and scraping across Levi's nerves. "Yeah, we keep this professional."

Levi smiled. They'd failed at keeping that one, spectacularly, but the other one… The other rule was the reason this partnership, this marriage had worked as well as it had from the start. "The other one, asshole."

Marsh righted his head, shook out his arms, and stretched his fingers, releasing the tension. A deep breath later, he repeated the four words he'd said to Levi that first morning at the bakery when they'd negotiated their marriage. "Don't lie to me."

"Turn around." Levi waited for him to do so, then closed the distance between them. "I did not lie to you. Hell, I didn't lie to Catherine either. I just couched my words in a way that hopefully she misinterpreted the same way you unfortunately did."

"How's that?"

He laid his hands on Marsh's chest. "That you aren't included in the list of those I will do anything to protect."

Marsh made the connection in less than a second, recalling Levi's exact words and realizing what he was saying. His eyes widened, a gasp escaping his parted lips. He lifted a hand to Levi's cheek. "Baby, I—"

Levi pressed three fingers over his lips. "We will not say those words to each other for the first time in some grimy back alley."

Marsh smiled behind his fingers. "I don't know, seems pretty perfect."

Perfect was his lips on Marsh's, tasting his smile, coaxing the last of the stress from him, reminding his husband that he was right there with him. "Believe me, Marsh. Believe this."

"I want to." Marsh dove back into the kiss and drew Levi with him against the wall, using it for support as they reconnected. They were both there. Together.

The pub's back door opened, startling them apart, and Levi laughed at seeing Sean there.

"What?" Sean said.

"Your timing is impeccable," Marsh grumbled.

"At least we got to kiss this time," Levi said.

Sean rolled his eyes. "Holt's got more info for us."

"It's what, four in the morning there?"

Marsh pushed off the wall and threw an arm over Levi's shoulder. "No one in that family sleeps. And?" he said to Sean.

"He confirmed Calex is one of Philippe's clients. He also confirmed that Calex is the lender on the Sixth Street Shelter."

"Holy shit," Levi cursed.

"Gets better," Sean said. "The federal minister of the

interior maintains a private family office in the same building as Calex here in Austria."

Marsh gasped. "Wagner's boss's boss?"

"Could be a coincidence."

Marsh scoffed. Levi didn't buy it either. "Six degrees of separation," he said. "We just need to tie Calex directly to Eder and to Catherine, and then we've got them. Extortion, blackmail, trafficking."

"To start," Marsh said with a wicked smirk, his confidence back where it belonged. "And I don't think we'll need to go to six."

THIRTY-TWO

"IT'S GORGEOUS UP HERE," Levi said as they walked down Grinzing's cobblestone streets. Vineyards covered the hillsides, houses looked like hobbit holes from the Shire, and taverns, shops, and biergartens lined the main streets.

"I wish I could have spent more time here," Marsh said. He vastly preferred this part of Vienna over the city proper, but work had kept him in town, close to the embassy.

"That's where you bought yours and Kwan's chess sets? In town?"

He nodded. "A craftsman who'd set up a shop in Stephansplatz. I carried a rollable one when I was in the service, but when I got here, the hand-carved boxes were everywhere. It was small enough to carry and a memento I could take with me always. I gave Kwan one as a thank you for helping me get the cyber legat gig."

They stopped in front of a glass-fronted shop on the main neighborhood square. On the other side of the picture window were all manner of hand-carved creations, including chess sets. And above the door was a hand-carved wooden sign with a familiar logo. "Looks like the right place," Marsh said.

The door opened, and a middle-aged man with neat brown hair, a long nose, and brown eyes behind his wire-rimmed spectacles stood over the threshold, smiling. "Can I help you with something?" he asked in German.

"Are you Harald Pincler?" Marsh replied. The man nodded. "Do you speak English?" He nodded again, and Marsh switched to English so Levi could follow the conversation. "I hope you can help," Marsh said. "I need to buy my new husband a chess set so he can practice."

"Herzlichen Glückwunsch!" the craftsman said with a wide smile, then remembered he was supposed to be speaking in English. "Congrats! How long have you been married?"

"A month," Levi answered.

"We're on our honeymoon," Marsh embellished. "We heard from friends we made at a pub last night that you're an amazing carpenter. We'd love to see your chess sets."

"Yes, let me show you." Harald showed him to the collection in the window and another stack in a bookcase beside it. Half a dozen or so, hand-carved board boxes and pieces with intricate inlays and plush velvet linings. As Levi gravitated to the ones with green touches, with double clasps for security, Marsh quickly sorted who he was shopping for and agreed whole-heartedly with Levi's selection.

"I think this one." He tapped the one currently in Levi's hands. "It's the right size to fit in your book bag." In David's book bag. "And it has an extra latch for safety so the pieces don't spill out." So there was less likelihood that when dropped it would pop open and explode. He traced his fingers over the narrow strips of green inlay. The same shade as David's eyes. "This is perfect." Levi glanced up, expression earnest, eyes glassy. "It's perfect," Marsh repeated, the "for David" unsaid but understood. He leaned in and kissed Levi's forehead.

Harald sighed, and Marsh glanced back over his shoulder, only to have Harald, likewise glassy-eyed, wave him off. "It's always a joy to see two people so in love."

"Thank you," Marsh said. "For your words and your skill." He gently slipped the set from Levi's fingers and held it out to Harald. "We'll take this one."

"Very good. One of my favorites." Harald moved behind the counter with the set, wrapping it securely in padded paper.

"How many of these do you make a year?" Levi asked.

"Each one is hand carved. It takes about a month, and I usually have a few going at a time."

"We're lucky to get one."

"Who's the most famous person you've sold a set to?" Marsh asked as he pulled the correct bills from his wallet.

Harald blew out a giant breath. "I don't know the most famous. I've been doing this for years. Actors filming in the area will stop by."

Marsh took back his change. "What about recently?"

"Oh, that's easy," Harald said as he finished wrapping the chess set and tucked it into a gift bag. "Charles Sanders. He's been a regular lately." He handed the bag to Levi, and Marsh hoped Harald didn't notice his husband's trembling hand. "He stopped by just the other day. Bought two."

"Two?" Marsh said. "Did he say for whom?"

"One he was flying all the way to America for a friend," Harald said excitedly. Marsh doubted he would remain so if he knew that box had almost killed two people. "The other is for a charity event this weekend."

THIRTY-THREE

AFTER AN INTENSE TWENTY-FOUR hours of meetings and strategy sessions with Wagner and Ross, with the teams in San Diego and Texas, with Charlie and her SAC in DC, not to mention the marathon hacking session with Holt, Jax, and Farmer, it was down to a single decision —make arrests now based on the evidence they had and stop any potential death and destruction at tomorrow's benefit or attend the benefit, gather more evidence, hope and pray they could divert any mayhem, and take Stefan Sanders into custody.

Marsh made his case for option one. "We have Calex, which Philippe confirmed is his client, and Catherine Sanders, who he admitted is his primary point of contact there." Marsh glanced across the penthouse dining table to Wagner. The poor guy looked worse than he had Monday morning; the shouting match with Philippe had been epic but had ended with both men in tears, their arms around each other. Wagner had been right. Philippe had had no idea what he'd gotten himself into. He'd just been trying to land a big fish so he could make enough money so Teddy could retire, live a less stressful life, and spend more time with him.

"Philippe also confirmed his design work for the family office of the federal minister of the interior, which was paid for with a tenant improvement allowance provided by their sublandlord, Calex. The sublease included a rent credit if any of the allowance was leftover, of which there had been two hundred fifty million. The minister signed that sublease one month after the U-Bahn bombing, for which we have Maria's sworn affidavit, testifying that Catherine Sanders blackmailed her brother to kill Stefan Sanders, and when he failed, blackmailed Maria to do the same.

"Finally, we have a sworn affidavit from JoJo that a recording of Catherine's voice matches the voice she heard threatening Greg Hudson that Calex would foreclose on the Sixth Street Shelter's mortgage if he didn't deliver the merchandise. Which we have probable cause to believe referred to victims that Eder's West Coast front, Orchard, was trafficking."

"Okay, that's all Calex and Catherine," Ross said as he scribbled furiously on a legal pad. "With a tangential connection to Orchard and Eder. I need more."

"Everything we had from Levi's case already. Stefan's presence at the Amarillo building, Catherine's signature on the purchase documents, and the chess boxes. Harald's affidavit that two boxes were sold directly to Charles Sanders and that one matches the description of the box delivered to Agent Kim."

Ross laid down his pencil and put his head together with Sean, the attorneys conferring. "Catherine's involvement with the bombing is your strongest case," Sean said after a moment. "But even then, it's not airtight. You've got a pillar of the community against testimony from a twenty-something-year-old under duress, who's family is living in poverty after what happened to her brother, who was mixed up with ISIS."

"And as for her brother," Ross picked up, "it's hearsay that Catherine gave him the kill order on Stefan, and then there's the question any good lawyer will use to kill the case… why did Peter still press that button if he didn't see Stefan on the platform?"

Marsh's frustration at the lawyer speak got the better of him, and the nagging question at the back of his mind escaped. "Why weren't you on the platform that night? Why did you take a car instead?"

All eyes turned to Ross. He didn't react defensively, just lowered his chin, his cheeks turning rosy beneath his dark skin. Embarrassment or regret? He lifted his chin after another moment and took a deep breath. "I'm surprised it took you so long to ask," he said. "Did you ever wonder why I shied away from the big events? And if I had to go, was in and out as quick as possible?"

"It's like you were allergic to them," Sean said.

"In a way, I am," Ross said. "I have social anxiety disorder. Those galas are my worst nightmare. I don't schmooze. I can't schmooze, not without breaking out in hives. And you know what Sophie was like, always the center of attention. If I'd taken that train, arrived there with her, I would have been a disaster."

"That's why you haven't climbed higher?" Levi asked.

He nodded. "I'm comfortable in this role. I'm comfortable working on smaller task force teams like this. Or in a pub hanging out with a few friends." He gestured around them. "And thankfully, I don't need to keep advancing. My wife makes triple what I do, and I'm more than okay with that."

"The year-end deposits?"

He nodded. "Tax planning."

"Why do you keep working at all?" Sean asked.

He chuckled. "I'd drive her crazy if I didn't. And I love my wife like you do your partners." He glanced around the table, and even Wagner nodded. "I got a second chance that night of the bombing. Sophie didn't. I want to solve this case and hold those responsible for her death accountable as much as you all do."

Sean clasped his shoulder. "Thank you for telling us."

It was not the explanation Marsh had expected but one that made sense, that answered the rest of the questions in his head tagged for Agent Ross. Understanding better how much he hated being the center of attention, Marsh moved them on. "What do we need to make the case less circumstantial?"

"Charles Sanders's prints," Sean said. "We need them to run against the partial prints forensics managed to get off the chess box delivered to Matt."

"You also need more direct ties between Calex and Eder," Ross said. "You've got it circumstantially, but you need—"

Marsh braced his hands on the table. "Greg or Amanda Hudson's testimony."

"Or Stefan's," Levi said. "Which is why we need to go to that benefit."

"We don't even know if he'll be there."

"Catherine said he would be."

"And we've got eyes on him in Salzburg," Wagner confirmed. "He's there."

The facilitator, the reason they were here in the first place, the crux of Levi's argument to let the benefit go on. "Give us your case," Sean said to him.

"We could make an arrest now, but given Eder's connections, the chances the charges will stick are not good."

"If we can even get charges brought," Wagner said. "I'll try, but it's ultimately not my call."

"Which means we would've shown our hand and lost the benefit of surprise, the chance to gather more evidence. Representative Anthony is on his way here." They'd still been up at two in the morning when the lead from Brax had come in; Marsh had hacked the flight manifest and confirmed it. "We observe, we see who he interacts with, how tight the Sanderses are with the minister of interior and anyone else. Sean, you cozy up to the bigwigs, I'll find Catherine and Stefan's parents, and Marsh, once we're on-site, you'll infiltrate the security system. Ross, you'll be in the comms van monitoring feeds. And we are prepared to take Stefan Sanders into custody at the end of the evening for questioning. Hopefully with the leverage we need.

"Wagner, your team will be on-site, investigating a bomb threat that is anonymously called in. Is there someone we can trust with the Federal Police in Salzburg?"

"A military mate," he suggested. "Not high enough up the ladder for Eder to corrupt, but high enough up to get us boots on the ground."

"Good. If we find that chess box, if we find it rigged, we tie the boxes and any prints on them to the chess boxes delivered stateside. Maybe it's the same person who Bell delivered the box to, who put the bomb inside it that killed him. Hard evidence either way."

The attorneys nodded.

"As long as we walk away from the night with no deaths and with Stefan Sanders in custody, we've not violated jurisdiction, we've got more leads to follow, and we've put a major crimp in Eder's criminal enterprise by detaining their facilitator."

"But there is a risk," Marsh said. "A big one in a tiny box that could go boom."

"We think. We don't know that."

He raised a brow.

"I know it's a risk, but it's a bigger risk letting these people continue to get away with what they do. I want this case to stick. I want this done. I want them shut down for good." He rounded the table and clasped Marsh's hand. "I want to go home with you and start our life together without these assholes and their threats hanging over us."

"Listen to your husband," Wagner said. "He's a smart man."

Conviction burned in Levi's eyes, all doubt gone. And for as many times as Levi had trusted him, trusted his intuition, Marsh went with his husband's gut on this one. "All right, then." He glanced over his shoulder at Ross and Wagner. "Where can we rent a couple of monkey suits on short notice?"

THIRTY-FOUR

THIS WAS the best balcony yet, hands down. "This view is incredible," Levi shouted back into the hotel room. Marsh was still in the bathroom dressing, so Levi returned his attention to Salzburg in all its glory. On the edge of what Marsh called the New City but was really the portion of town built in the 1800s, hardly new, their hotel overlooked the Salzach River. Fronting the other side of the river was a row of colorful buildings, the delicate pastel tones reminding Levi of cake frosting, the large baroque church of the Old City behind them, and the medieval fortress up the hill. And if he looked left or right instead of across, all he saw were rolling hills of green and the Alps. "I want to bring David here. Hell, I want to come back here some time when we're not working so we can enjoy it."

"Magical was my thought the first time I visited here."

Magical was Marsh in a tuxedo. Sean knew a tailor, of course, and every inch of the black-and-white ensemble fit Marsh like a glove. Except the tie, which hung loose around his neck, but Levi figured that was more Marsh's resistance than the suit. He liked the tiny imperfection, made the rest of the perfect package—tamed dark hair, broad shoulders and chest, long legs—even more divine.

"Do not lick your lips at me." Marsh plucked his phone off the charger and joined him on the balcony. "We need to call David, and then we need to get going. We do not need to end up sweaty and in bed."

"Yet."

Marsh smirked. "Yet."

They stood against the balcony rail, the Old City behind them, and rang David. He answered the video call, and as soon as it connected, his ginger brows raced north. "Ohmigod! Am I missing the wedding redo?"

"If there is a redo," Levi said, "you'll be there."

Irina poked her face into the frame. "Us too!"

"Yes," Marsh said. "Everyone can be at the second wedding, I promise."

"Whereabouts?"

"Our backyard," David told Irina. "The view is perfect, we've got a fire pit, a huge table, and this massive tree…"

As he carried on, Levi struggled around the knot in his throat, struggled not to get teary-eyed when he looked at Marsh and saw him struggling too. Struggling with happiness neither of them knew what to do with but that they both wanted to share with their loved ones. They shared a nod, an agreement, a promise.

"Are you in Salzburg?" The question drew Levi's attention back to the screen, where Irina had disappeared, leaving just David sitting at the kitchen table.

He cleared his throat. "We are." He ducked his head to the side so David could get a better view. "Take a look at this place." He moved the camera side to side, giving him a look up and down the river and at the Old City. "We want to come back here with you sometime."

"Looks old."

"It is," Marsh said. "It was founded in AD 696. That fortress up there"—he jutted a thumb over his shoulder—"is from the medieval era, and the church in the Old City at the bottom of the hill is from the 1600s."

He looked mildly intrigued. Levi sealed the deal. "Food is pretty delicious too. Our late lunch was a fresh-baked pretzel, salami, and a chocolate torte."

David rubbed his hands together. "Now we're talking!"

"Everything good there?" Marsh asked once they were done laughing.

David nodded, then leaned closer to the screen, voice lowered. "I think maybe Holt is tired of the desert. He's very red."

More laughter before a serious turn, even if David didn't understand how serious. "And, like, all his siblings and their friends are here," he carried on. "They're scary, but I don't think anyone is getting through them." Or maybe he did understand and was just that comfortable. Felt that safe. A good sign.

A good call Marsh had made, calling in reinforcements in case Eder made a play while they were making theirs.

"When are you coming home?" David asked, voice losing some of its cheer.

Levi understood the feeling. Salzburg was magical and all, but he'd give anything to be on his back patio, sharing breakfast casserole with his son and husband. "If all goes according to plan, early next week."

David brightened. "Both of you?" he asked, an optimistic ring to his tone.

"Both of us."

"You're still being careful?"

Marsh leaned in closer. "I've got his back, David."

He was convinced enough that his curiosity about the chocolate torte Levi mentioned won out, asking for details that they gave him before Holt jumped on the line for a quick status check. All was in order, Mi Herencia more than secure. They hung up, Levi feeling more hopeful than ever about wrapping this up soon and the future that awaited them back in the States, but he didn't want to presume. He pocketed his phone and looked out at the river, afraid that if he looked at Marsh, his husband would see the lie, how badly he wanted what David had proposed. "So about that wedding we just promised your moms and David. If you don't—"

Marsh grasped his chin and forced his gaze. "I want," he said, the same look in his eyes that Levi imagined was in his too.

"I do too."

Marsh brushed their lips together, soft and hopeful, that tempting taste of the future Levi couldn't get enough of. He drew back first and took Levi's hand in his, thumb rubbing across his ring. "We get through tonight, we bring Stefan in and get him to flip, we close this case and shut Eder down, and then there's nothing I want more than to spend the rest of my life with you."

A knock sounded on the door.

Levi snickered. "Sean?"

Marsh rolled his eyes. "The king of interruptions strikes again." He walked to the door, Levi on his heels, and it was a good thing he was close, the surprise enough to make Levi put a hand to Marsh's back to catch his balance.

"Ma—" he started, then corrected. "Kwan, what are you doing here?" His ASAC was on a tuxedoed Sean's arm, hair swept up in a chignon, decked out in a long silver sheath dress and heels that could pass as murder weapons.

"Eagle," Marsh greeted. "This is a pleasant surprise."

"Nerd," she said with a smirk. "I thought you might need this." She drew her other hand from behind her back, Marsh's snow-white Stetson balanced on it. "Can't have you going to a fancy gala without your best hat."

Marsh took it from her reverently, a nod of thanks, and placed it on his head, and if Levi hadn't already been confident about tonight's outcome, seeing that hat back on his husband's head, where it belonged, he was certain. They'd be back where they belonged soon.

THIRTY-FIVE

MARSH OFFERED Levi a hand out of the car, seeing him to his feet and guiding him away from the curb, making sure he didn't trip or run into anyone while his attention was focused on the castle in front of them. Because really, there was no other word for the yellow structure built into the hill, its turrets and towers soaring above a sprawling mansion and even more sprawling manicured grounds. Levi's "Whoa" was one hundred percent justified.

And a reminder Marsh couldn't help but poke fun at. "Okay, Keanu."

"If the 'whoa' fits." Levi shot him a sideways grin before staring up at the castle again. "It's massive."

"They're probably the richest people in town," Sean said as he and Julia began to move forward at the urging of the valets who were impatient to keep the line of cars moving.

Music drifted outside from the grand foyer, beckoning guests into the marble spectacle under glass chandeliers— three of them the space was so huge. And splashed with photo banners and easel pictures of refugees, shots of suffering families huddled in front of Eder-branded tents, in Eder-branded thermal blankets, soup bowls and canteens in their hands.

"Are they fucking kidding?" Levi cursed under his breath.

"You've seen Marsh's maps," Sean said. "Capital flows into these places earmarked for refugee efforts."

"And then it gets redirected elsewhere," Marsh continued. "Laundered through bitcoin and other means to be used by trafficking empires. They may have helped that kid"—he pointed at one of the children pictured on a banner—"but they destroyed the lives of dozens of others."

Levi turned away from the pictures and closed his eyes, breathing deep. "I think I'm going to be sick."

Marsh laid a hand on his lower back. "Just focus on bringing them down."

"I knew all this, but seeing the hypocrisy on full display… I didn't feel this sick in Texas."

Marsh gave him a moment to recover and checked in with the rest of their team. "Wagner, Ross, do you copy?"

"I can hear you," Ross radioed. "Just need some eyes now."

"Roger that. Wags?"

"I'm—" the inspector started, but Marsh tuned him out when he saw who was making a beeline their direction.

"Agents," Catherine greeted, "so delighted you could make it. And Mr. Henby-Paxton, you brought a plus-one, who I don't believe is your wife."

"Assistant Special Agent in Charge Julia Kwan." She held out her hand, and damned if Catherine didn't hesitate for a moment. "I hope it's not too much of an inconvenience." Someone hadn't reported in. Julia was a surprise. A point in the win column for them.

"Of course not." Catherine recovered and shook her hand. "Your former colleague purchased an entire table with his matching grant."

"Paxton is committed to relieving the refugee crisis," Sean said. "And I'm personally committed, having seen the effects of traffickers who take advantage."

Catherine pulled a face similar to the one her assistant had the other day. Marsh would title this one, *Fake British Woman Smelling Shit*. As if she could hear him, she turned her sneer on Marsh. "If you don't mind, Agent Marshall, I need to steal your husband for a moment."

"Well, in fact I—"

"You need to go wrangle your pet inspector," she said. "He barged in here a half hour before guests started to arrive, raving about a bomb."

"Did he now?"

"He's in the scullery downstairs." She looped her arm through Levi's, and it was everything Marsh could do not to rip those evil hands off his man. Levi's calm nod—they'd expected this, he was prepared—was all that kept Marsh from flying off the handle.

And Sean reiterating the same as Catherine led Levi away toward the atrium courtyard where more guests were gathered. "We knew this would happen," Sean said. "He'll be safe in the crowd there, and we'll keep eyes on. Go find Wagner while she's distracted and hook into the system. Get Ross some eyes too."

"You ready to listen to me now?" Wagner said in his ear.

Marsh closed his eyes and inhaled deep. Reset. His husband could handle himself and Catherine. He needed to work on the other threat and focus on shutting Eder down for good. "Tell me how to get to the scullery."

He was at the top of the stairs to the downstairs kitchen when one of the wildcards they'd considered appeared. Hair cut and neatly styled, tuxedo freshly tailored, Binu Patel looked a sight better than when Marsh had last seen him, but the ghost still lingered in the bags under his eyes and his sunken cheeks, in the slump of his shoulders and his near-empty champagne glass.

"We figured you might be here," Marsh said

"Every major political player in the region is in there." He gestured with his glass to the teeming courtyard. "Where else would I be?"

Marsh couldn't stop the scoff escaping. "Is that why you're here?"

Binny stepped closer, a hand clasping Marsh's bicep, and lowered his voice. "We're after the same thing here."

"I sincerely doubt that."

"They'll find your weakness and use it."

"Is that what she did to you? Is that how Catherine Sanders made you her spy?"

He released Marsh's arm and stepped back, and Marsh could swear that was hurt in his hard dark stare. "I don't work for her." He drained the rest of his champagne, and when his gaze returned to Marsh, it was carefully devoid again. "Don't let him be a weakness. We have too many pawns on the board already. Use their pieces. Make them come to us. That's the only way any of us survive this."

THIRTY-SIX

"HOW WAS THE TRIP INTO SALZBURG?" Catherine asked as she led Levi into the bustling open-air courtyard that was the size of the entire downstairs floor of his home in San Diego. Little white lights wrapped the trunk of every tree and stretched out through their branches while additional fixture lights on the second-floor balconies cast the space, its fountain, and the dozens of tables with guests gathered around them, in soft inviting light.

"Lovely," he answered Catherine as much to her question as a commentary on the current surroundings. Hostess excluded.

Judging by her flirtatious laugh, she misread him once again. "And our little village?"

"I don't think I'd call it little, but it is amazing. Magical. I'd like my son to visit someday."

"You two are close?"

He and Marsh had anticipated this line of questioning. It was the most obvious leverage against him, and Levi had already opened that door in their previous conversation.

No use hiding the ball now. "He matters more to me than anyone."

"That's good to hear. There's someone I want you to meet." She led them closer to the fountain, toward a large crowd gathered around one of the tables. "Let me introduce you to our guest of honor."

The crowd parted, and by the table next to the fountain stood Charles Sanders, a big man, tall and regal but in no way a matchstick, no hair on top of his head, all of it on his chin, and all of it white. And beside him stood Representative Stewart Anthony, his salt-and-pepper hair neatly trimmed, his blue eyes bright, and his smile the practiced political one Levi hated. No, on second thought, Sean would never be able to pull that off. He was too genuine a person.

He faked a stutter step; Catherine bought it, laughing at his feigned surprise. "I promised you could meet my uncle tonight, and I'm sure your sources already told you the good congressman would be here as well."

"Ah, there she is," Charles said, beaming as he waved his niece closer.

Anthony's smile for her seemed more genuine, fraternal almost. The nickname certainly was. "Catt, you look amazing as always."

"Stewart," she greeted warmly, leaning in to kiss each of his cheeks. "I'm glad you made it on time.

"Short hold-up at Dulles, but we worked it out." He picked his glass back up and took a swallow of champagne. "And who's this? Your date?"

"Sadly, no." She pouted, the look completely wrong on her, the act completely wrong, and an act, Levi was sure, but hell if Charles and Anthony weren't buying it. "He's married to someone I believe you know. This is Special Agent Levi Bishop, Special Agent Emmitt Marshall's husband."

Anthony nearly spit out his champagne. "Well, that's a surprise."

Catherine looped an arm through Levi's, pulling him closer. "I'm winning him over to our side. Uncle Charles, this is Levi."

"It's nice to meet you both." Levi extended his hand, and both men were too well mannered not to take it. And too distracted to notice the very thin hardly noticeable film covering Levi's hand. Prints obtained, Levi withdrew his hand and put it behind his back, not wanting to compromise the valuable evidence.

"I hear you've been causing us some trouble," Charles said, reclaiming his own glass.

"Only the *if you do crime, you do time* kind," Levi said with a wink.

Everyone laughed, Anthony's nervous, Charles's and Catherine's with the air of confidence that came from decades of getting away with it.

Charles leaned into the lie. "No do-crime kind here. As you can see, we're a philanthropic organization." He gestured around the courtyard and at the foyer. "Everyone is here tonight to support bringing humanitarian aid to refugees." He laid a hand on Anthony's forearm. "My old friend here has promised your government's cooperation and funding."

"Your old friend?"

"You remember the Diplomatic Academy from the other day?" Catherine said.

He nodded.

"This old man"—Anthony clicked his glass against Charles's—"used to play chess in the courtyard there every Thursday with one of my professors. Taught me to play."

"You were a student there?" Levi didn't remember seeing that in his record.

"Briefly. For a summer. We were supposed to be in Innsbruck, but there was a last-minute change in venue."

"A change I will forever be grateful for." Charles considered him fondly.

Like a son.

"He considers him a son," Marsh echoed in his ear. It was a jolt, the comm clicking on so suddenly, but Levi managed to hide his reaction, in large part because the picture before him had just snapped into perfect clarity.

Same as it had for Marsh. "He's the heir."

"If you'll excuse us," Catherine said, interrupting their thoughts. "I need to get Agent Bishop back to his husband before the cowboy comes gunning for us all."

He said his goodbyes to Charles and Anthony, the two of them getting sucked into conversations with other guests while Catherine led him to the quieter edge of the courtyard. She snagged two glasses from a passing server and held one out to him. "Do you see now?"

"That you're not second in line but third." He sipped from the glass. "Must sting."

She smiled, tapping the rim of her glass against her ruby lips. "I do like you, Agent Bishop. You cut right to the chase, so I'll do you the favor of the same. I intend to be the queen before this night is over." She leaned forward, kissing each of his cheeks as she'd done Anthony. Whispering in his ear before she drew back. "If you join me, I'll make sure the team I have waiting outside Mi Herencia delivers David to you in one piece." She stepped back and held her glass up in a toast. "And breathing."

Levi clicked the rim of his glass against hers, praying his whole world was not about to shatter. "We do what we have to do."

THIRTY-SEVEN

LEVI MADE it to the scullery, barely, his legs wobbly, his breathing erratic, every worst-case scenario running through his head, even though they'd planned for all of them, had the reinforcements in place to make sure none of those worst cases came to pass. Didn't silence the father in him screaming to get to his son, to make sure he was safe. He put out a hand to catch himself on the door.

"Don't do that." Marsh looped an arm around his waist, taking his weight, steadying him. "I've got you."

"David," he choked out.

"I've already alerted Holt. Nothing is getting through that perimeter. Between the Madigan and Redemption forces, Barnes's FBI team, and my mothers, David is in the safest place he can be right now. Trust me." Levi nodded and sucked in a breath, trying to wrangle his emotions. "Now let Wags get that film off your hand."

He held out his right hand, and Wagner carefully removed the coating with a pair of forceps. He held it up to the light and smiled. "We got it."

"And did we get enough from Catherine?" Levi asked.

"We're getting there," Ross answered from the laptop screen open on the scullery island.

"Sean and Julia?"

"Chatting up the minister of interior." Ross flipped the feed from him to a shot of the courtyard, Sean and Julia standing with a dark-haired man in full uniform, a stone's throw from Charles and Anthony.

"There's more," Marsh said. "Binny's here too."

Levi rested his head on his husband's shoulder. Not unexpected, but a lot of pieces on the board to keep track of. And what about the most important one? "Any sign of Stefan yet?"

Ross, back on camera, shook his head. "No sign of their parents either."

"Catherine means to eliminate him."

"And Anthony," Marsh said, "By the sound of it."

"We've got movement out front," a German voice said over the comms, Wagner's Salzburg contact.

In the scullery, all of them huddled around the laptop, and Marsh took control of the feeds and flipped quickly to the front cameras. Stefan Sanders emerged from a black SUV, and appearing behind him were Henry and Anna Sanders, his and Catherine's parents.

But neither Stefan nor his parents were the most interesting, most potentially dangerous new arrival. "Is that what I think it is?" Levi asked.

Marsh leaned closer to the screen. "The chess set from Charles's desk in Stefan's hands." He straightened, his expression grim. "Ross, do you have the background info on their parents? What do they do?"

"Hold a second."

They'd only recently begun to take a deep dive into the estranged half of the Sanders clan. Had been unable to make contact to learn more about what had precipitated that estrangement. Hadn't poked around too much locally either or asked Wagner's contact to do so for fear of tipping off Eder.

Ross came back on the line. "Anna's a teacher. Henry is a—" He closed his eyes, defeat written all over his features. "Fuck me. Henry Sanders is a painter now, relatively prominent. But before they immigrated he worked for a mining company. Corporate, but his degree was in—"

"Engineering," Marsh said. "Explosives, I would bet." He opened a terminal window and typed commands Levi didn't understand, but it only took a minute before a service record appeared. "He served. Not in an explosives ordinance unit but he had the marks to do so if he'd wanted. Was a better mechanical engineer."

"Is that why they're estranged?" Pieces flew together in Levi's head. "He wanted out of the family business, went straight, left Austria, but his brother kept calling in deadly favors, even across the pond."

Marsh was nodding. "The person Bell took Kwan's chess box to. Who Anthony brought the one from here to. He rigged them both."

"And now he's rigged another box, at Catherine's request. At Stefan's, who is trying to get them clear." That theory had always rung true with the parent and son in Levi. Made sense why Stefan would ally himself with Sophie, and then, when that path was closed off, with Catherine. Why he couldn't risk his and Marsh's reappearance threatening his parents' escape.

"That's what Sophie was after," Marsh said with a nod. "What Binny is after."

"But he took Catherine's deal instead."

There was only one way out of this. "We need to make him a better deal."

THIRTY-EIGHT

MARSH AND LEVI slid into their seats at the Paxton table in the middle of the grand ballroom, just as Charles Sanders tapped the mic behind the podium that had been set up on a raised dais at the front of the space. "Is this thing on?"

Marsh lifted the brim of his cap and wiped at the sweat that had collected around his hairline over the past forty minutes of frantic maneuvers—physical intercepts, calls with trusted partners at umpteen different agencies, complicated negotiations. Tears shed and contingencies put into play. Levi wasn't doing much better, shrugging out of his coat, the back of his dress shirt sweat drenched. There'd been some close calls. Was it enough?

Levi leaned close to him, voice lowered. "He's like Kris Kringle, the awful one they never tell you about as a kid."

That was exactly what Charles Sanders was like beyond just the appearance. An evil specter that kept adults in line more than kids—through blackmail, addiction, and murder.

Through a smokescreen of hypocrisy that was on full display this evening. "I'd like to welcome you all here tonight and thank you for joining us. We at Eder Capital are committed to delivering aid to refugees around the world, and your donations, your capital investments, make this important work possible. When you put your money and trust in us, you know it is going to a socially responsible business partner, one who is as committed to making the world a better place as you are."

Levi gripped his knee beneath the table, his expression green around the gills again. Marsh understood the I'm-gonna-puke feeling.

"Before we start the dinner and program portion of the evening, we do have some special guests with us that I'd like to honor." He waited for a spotlight to flick on, then hand over his eyes, pretended to be looking for someone… at their table. "Mr. Henby-Paxton, where are you?"

Sean cursed under his breath—"He damn well knows exactly where I am"—and stood, the spotlight shining on him.

"There you are," Charles feigned surprise and graciousness well. "Mr. Henby-Paxton is the CEO of Paxton Industries, and he's generously pledged to match tonight's donations with a grant to Polaris for their nonprofit work to combat human trafficking."

The crowd applauded politely, and Sean, after a gracious nod, sank back into his chair.

"With us tonight are also my brother and his family." The spotlight shifted to the round table at the front of the ballroom. To Henry and Anna who looked as green as Levi. "It's been some time since we shared a meal together, and I look forward to doing that with you tonight."

"And finally, our guest of honor. Stewart, join me up here." Anthony rose from his chair at the main table and practically bounded onto the stage, a real smile for Charles, then a politician's one when he turned to the crowd. "I met Representative Anthony thirty years ago when he studied here in Vienna." He clasped his shoulder, every bit the proud surrogate father. "I knew this was a man who would do great things. And he was a man I could beat at chess." The crowd laughed, Anthony too. "He's like a son to me. He's been with me on this humanitarian endeavor over the decades, and I will be thrilled to throw my support behind him when he officially announces his candidacy for president of the United States." Camera's flashed and partygoers applauded, all but those at Marsh's table who'd watched Anthony fearmonger his way to the top, spewing hate at people like them. "Stefan, if you'll please."

Stefan rose, the chess box in one hand, his mother grasping the other. He kissed her knuckles, then briefly clasped his father's hand as well as he passed them on the way to the stage.

Catherine sat up straighter.

Stefan handed the box to Charles.

Sweat dripped down Marsh's neck. Had they done enough? Had Catherine made another play after theirs? Was Stefan making plays no one knew about?

Levi's hand, still on his knee, gripped tighter.

"You will always be my favorite person to meet across the board." Charles handed him the box, the two men hugging over it.

Anthony drew back and sniffled. "The feeling is completely mutual." He turned to the audience, making his pitch. "Some of you may know, I didn't have a dad growing up. I got one when I turned twenty, and he is my staunchest supporter and fiercest competitor. This"—he held the box to his chest—"means the world to me. And I hope it'll sit on the Resolute desk one day soon."

"Well, open it damn it," Charles said with a watery chuckle. "The craftsmanship is remarkable."

He flipped the latch, Catherine leaned forward, and Marsh held his breath, hand over Levi's.

"It's beautiful." Anthony beamed as he looked inside the box and held a piece up for the audience to see.

Without incident. Without the bought and paid for explosion.

The would-be murderess's expression was the opposite of Anthony's. Barely contained fury as her gaze whipped to their table. Then whipped the opposite direction, the closest set of doors swinging open and Wagner leading a group of officers to her table. "Catherine Sanders, you're under arrest."

"For what?" she protested as Wagner hauled her up.

"The attempted murder of Charles Sanders, Stefan Sanders, and Stewart Anthony." More surprised gasps from the crowd, not the good kind. "I'm sure we'll add more charges," Wagner said as he put the cuffs on Catherine. "But those three are the biggies."

Charles and Anthony stood on the dais, silent, a calculating look about them Marsh did not like. That made him wonder what they had missed. For his part, Stefan had rejoined his quietly sobbing parents while the minister of the interior met Wagner at the back doors and demanded to know what was going on.

"We'll fill you in at the station, sir."

He kicked open the door, but not before Catherine wheeled around in his arms, seething, shouting back at Marsh's table, at her family's, at her uncle, brother, and surrogate cousin onstage. "You won't win. None of you."

THIRTY-NINE

A MAJOR CANDIDACY ANNOUNCEMENT. A foiled assassination attempt. A high-profile figure arrested for attempting to murder her uncle, brother, and said candidate. All in a room full of witnesses and press. It was a mess —and for once, not Levi's job to clean up. He and Marsh had given their statements; Wagner and his Salzburg counterpart were processing the scene and a lawyered-up Catherine; Stefan was in custody, a deal struck with Charlie's help stateside that would extradite him back to the US on lesser organized crime charges in exchange for testimony, clear reentry for his parents, and minor charges against his father; and Ross, Sean, and Kwan were sorting out how to explain the US team's involvement without compromising the present charges and the broader case they were continuing to build.

Phase two complete.

Levi finished showering, spent an extra minute drying off with the sinfully soft hotel towels, then, fluffy softness wrapped around his waist, followed the low rumble of his husband's voice into the hotel bedroom. Marsh was in a similar freshly showered state, towel stretched across his muscled thighs, barely covering the goods Levi wanted to get at, as he leaned against the wrought iron headboard, a pillow at his back, the phone to his ear. "That's perfect," he said. "Don't tell David, though. I want it to be a surprise, and I want to be sure we're clear."

Levi cocked a brow, then a knee, his towel falling to the floor as he climbed onto the bed and straddled Marsh's lap.

"Gotta go, Brax," Marsh said, and given the gravel in his voice, if Brax didn't know why his best friend was disconnecting in a hurry, he wasn't as smart a man as Levi gave him credit for. Marsh's cheeks flamed bright red. Yep, Brax knew. "I plan to." He disconnected the call and tossed the phone onto the bedside table next to Levi's.

"Two questions," Levi said as he worked free the knot of Marsh's towel.

"I only have one." Marsh raked his gaze down Levi's body, smirking when Levi's semi hardened more. "But you can go first."

"Well, aren't you considerate." Ignoring the prize revealed, for now, Levi ran his hands up his husband's chest, slowly, lightly, teasing touches that made Marsh squirm, made him strain for more. "One, what aren't we telling David?"

"That we have plane tickets booked, and that if all goes to plan, we'll be home by Monday."

Levi smiled, a full happy one, no hiding his joy at that news. They'd had to exercise some contingencies but not all of them, and he prayed it stayed that way. That they could get back home to their family, to the life they were building together. To see the same joy, the same hope reflected on

Marsh's face magnified Levi's happiness tenfold. He framed Marsh's cheeks, tracing the corners of his bright beautiful smile. "Fuck, you're gorgeous."

"Says the bombshell naked in my lap." He bent his knees, bumping Levi forward, his erection pressing against Marsh's abs, Marsh's cock a tempting ridge beneath him. "Second question so I can ask mine?"

Levi draped himself over Marsh, hands braced on the headboard, lips at his ear. "What did Brax say to make you blush like that?"

Marsh's hands were warm on his skin, one burning a path to his lower back, holding their bodies close together, the other languidly climbing his spine. "That I should spend tomorrow in bed with my husband."

"Your bestie is a smart man." Levi licked into the hollow beneath his ear and got a roll of Marsh's hips in return, his erection skating the underside of Levi's balls and taint. "What was your question?"

The hand on his back crept higher, into his hair, cradling his skull and tipping back his head. "What do you need tonight?"

"My husband." As simple as that.

Marsh cradled his cheek. "I felt like your husband tonight."

"Because you are my husband." Levi mimicked the gesture Marsh was so fond of, covering his hand and running his thumb over Marsh's wedding band. "You have been for weeks. You just have to believe me."

Fear swirled with desire in Marsh's dark eyes. With that something more Levi felt in his chest too, the words on the tip of his tongue. Marsh tried to speak them first. "I believe you. I lo—" He closed his eyes, pressed his lips together, so used to shutting the thought down. But Levi was there to catch it, to return it. Was as ready as Marsh to start their future together. To look love in the face again.

"Trust me, baby," Levi urged. "Trust me with the words and with this." He pressed his hand over Marsh's heart. "With all of you."

FORTY

MARSH HAD NEVER BEEN MORE frightened in his life. Not the first time he was bullied. Not the day his mom packed them in the car and left his father. Not his first day of basic training, not the day his first love broke his heart, not the day he watched a building come down on two of his friends. Not even the day he stood under an arch of flowers and said I do.

No, this right here was far more terrifying. The hardest moment of his life, one he'd sworn off, determined not to put his heart back out there again to be rejected. Cursed.

But Levi had broken that curse, had said so himself. Was sitting on his lap ready to take his late wife's advice and look love in the face again. Marsh was ready too.

He swallowed hard and opened his eyes. Gazed at his husband, the bravest man he'd ever met. No, this wasn't the hardest moment of Marsh's life. It was the easiest. "I love you."

Levi's smile was as magical as any city Marsh had ever set foot in. "I love you too."

Tasted better than any food he'd ever put in his mouth too, their lips meeting in a kiss that would have quickly gone from soft to plundering if not for their giant smiles.

"I have another question," Marsh said.

"What's that?"

"What do you need from your husband tonight?"

Levi kissed him once more, then righted himself, and there was the fire, burning in blue eyes so intense, so hungry Marsh would've hauled Levi back to him if he hadn't canted sideways instead. He opened the bedside table drawer and pulled out two items.

The lube he tossed on the bed.

The handcuffs he held in front of Marsh.

"I need you to use me. I need you to be rough. To not hold back. To show me how much you love me. Can you do that for me?"

Marsh clasped his hips, held him down, and rocked his hips up, rutting his erection against Levi's taint. "Now who's the bad Bishop?"

"Except I'm not trapped with you." Levi braced both hands on his chest, the cold metal causing Marsh to hiss. Levi's kiss to his sternum, the roll of his hips, the precome streaked across his abs causing him to groan. "This, you, are freedom. You rescued me from the darkness. You got me back in the game, the whole board, the future, in front of us." Levi stretched over him and cuffed his own wrist to the metal bed frame. "Now show me what our future holds. Together."

Marsh angled his head, rewarded Levi's trust with kisses from his cuffed wrist, down the inside of his arm, to the crook of his neck, Levi shivering, goose bumps rising all over his skin. Marsh returned to his mouth, murmuring,

"Yeah, baby, I can do that," before capturing his lips in the plundering kiss their earlier soft ones had promised.

He sucked, he nibbled, he swept his tongue through every corner of Levi's mouth. Wanting it all. Wanting all the secret parts of Levi. He rolled out from under him, flipped him, and trailed his chin down Levi's spine, letting the rough stubble scrape. Levi whimpered and thrust against the mattress. Writhed more as Marsh gave one then the other ass cheek the same rough treatment. Focused all his effort on the twin divots at the top of his crack.

First with his beard, then his mouth.

Traveled lower with his tongue. Not gentle. Rough, claiming, demanding, lashing over Levi's rim and spearing into his hole. And Levi loved every second, groaning, clutching the pillow with his free hand, trying to ram his ass back for more but limited by the cuff that rattled against the headboard.

Marsh moved in closer, making it easier for Levi, keeping it rough, increasing the friction, but giving Levi what he needed, rewarding his trust. Grabbing the lube and working him open with slick fingers. Driving Levi crazy, causing him to hump the bed with lovely abandon. "Fuck, what are you doing to me?"

"Loving you." Marsh, though, would rather be loving on another part of him that needed his attention. He drew back and tapped Levi's hip. "Up, baby. I'll give you something better to ride."

He must have been anticipating Marsh's cock because his surprised expression when Marsh slid face-first between his spread legs was fucking priceless. "Fuck, I wish I had a camera right now." To capture that face. And the sight of his flushed, heaving, turned the hell on husband above him.

He kept watch as he stretched his lips around Levi's cock and treated him to the same torture he'd exacted on Marsh in the shower in Texas. Licking, teasing, swallowing him inch by inch. Until Marsh had Levi buried to the hilt in his mouth. He slapped his hip and mumbled, "Ride," around his cock.

Levi gasped, clutched the headboard with both hands, and thrust.

Pounded into Marsh's mouth, bringing tears to Marsh's eyes, bringing relief to a heart that had been second best for so long but now beat as one with the man above him.

"Baby, I'm going to come."

Marsh squeezed his ass, and Levi exploded in his mouth.

Came down in slow languid thrusts as Marsh licked him clean, then scooted the rest of the way up against the headboard. Putting Levi back on his lap where the evening had started. Where Marsh had wanted it to go all along. He peppered his husband's face with kisses, told him how amazing he was, how beautiful he was when he fell apart, how hard he'd fallen for him.

How much he loved him.

Marginally recovered, Levi righted himself and palmed Marsh's face. "Let me show you how much I love you too." He rose on his knees and reached behind himself with his free hand, grabbing one cheek. "Help me out, Mr. Levi Bishop," he said with a grin. Marsh kissed his chin, grasped his husband's other ass cheek, and Levi sank down on him in one fluid motion. Tight slick heat all around him and draped across his front too, Levi determined to make this ride a longer, smoother one. "Make love to me, husband."

Like magnets, their lips gravitated back together and

stayed that way, brushing, angling, opening as their lower bodies rocked together, Marsh pumping into Levi, and Levi riding him like they had all the time in the world.

The night, that future he spoke of stretched out before them.

He wrapped his arms around Levi, holding him close, wanting to keep him there forever. "This wasn't supposed to happen. I wasn't supposed to fall in love. But I did. And I do. So fucking much, Levi."

Levi's eyes gleamed with happy wetness. "I do too."

By the time Marsh finally came, a fierce quiet explosion, his come filling Levi's ass, his silent scream swallowed by his husband's gentle kiss, his tears combining with Levi's, he was as wrecked by Levi's gentle lovemaking as Levi was by the rough tumbling and as certain as he'd ever been that he'd finally put his trust, his heart in the hands of the right person.

The best person he'd ever known.

His husband.

FORTY-ONE

THE BANGING on the hotel room door started at six the next morning.

Marsh turned away from the sunrise over the Salzach River, from the view that had once been magical but was a new shade of haunted this morning.

They'd expected this, had thought last night that maybe they'd escaped it, but here they were, exercising the rest of their contingencies. Planning didn't make reality any easier, didn't make the moves they had to execute any less difficult.

Some of the hardest in chess. The hardest they'd face in their careers.

And in their marriage.

He crossed the room to the door and swung it open to an uncharacteristically disheveled Binu Patel. Jacket askew, vest unbuttoned, tie undone, too many hairs out of place for Marsh to count. But the fire in Binny's dark eyes, the life in him, was more than Marsh had seen this entire visit.

The legat charged into the room, voice raised, gesturing

wildly. "Catherine Sanders is out on bail. Her pal, her lover, the minister of the interior, pulled some strings. The Federal Police released her into the custody of Special Agent Levi Bishop five fucking hours ago."

"Binny," Marsh started, but Binny was ranting again while looking all around the room. For someone or something. Evidence probably. Which he wouldn't find.

"There's surveillance footage of them leaving the country together." He shoved his phone under Marsh's nose, video playing of Catherine and Levi boarding a train to Munich. "They used fake passports." He snatched back his phone. "And despite being told to stay in the country, Charles Sanders is on a private plane with Stewart Anthony, flying to DC. All of them gone! Do you have any idea how many months—years—of work you and your husband have ruined?"

Marsh left Binny ranting and went to the in-room safe, opening it and pulling out the invite from last night's gala.

"I told you not to let him be a weakness."

"He's not my weakness," Marsh said. "He's my strength." And he had to trust that strength, had to trust that Levi would keep his promises and hold true to their vows.

He returned to Binny, who stood still and stopped shouting long enough to notice the second ring on Marsh's hand. "Is that his ring?"

"He left it for me." He held the card out to Binny. "With this. Flip it over."

Binny flipped the card and read Levi's chicken-scratch out loud. "King hunt."

"This is phase three," Marsh said, even as his gut tossed and turned.

They'd planned for this, but letting the love of his life go, letting him venture into the center of the board was the most painful, most frightening thing he'd ever done. The worst day of his life. But it had been Levi's choice. "Romantic chess and all that," he'd said with a parting kiss goodbye. A desperado sacrifice to bring this dangerous game they were playing to an end.

"We captured their rook." Marsh swallowed hard around the knot of fear in his throat. "The facilitator is ours. We captured their queen too, even if she doesn't know it yet. Now, we lure their king to our side of the board. Into our territory."

Binny's rage face cracked, realization dawning. "And check."

"And check." If all went according to plan. Marsh fisted his hand with two rings, running his thumb over Levi's, and vowed to do whatever it took to make that happen. To end this game and keep his promises—bring Levi home, give their families that wedding redo, and spend the rest of his life loving his husband.

Want to know how it all ends?
Marsh & Levi's story concludes in *King Hunt*,
coming Spring 2023!
Preorder Now

For all the latest updates on new projects, sneak peeks, and more, sign up for Layla's Newsletter

and join the Layla's Lushes Reader Group on
Facebook.

Reviews are an invaluable tool when it comes to spreading
the word about great reads. Please consider leaving an
honest review for *Bad Bishop* on your favorite review site.

Thank you for reading!

ACKNOWLEDGMENTS

Thank you, readers, for joining me again on this wild and crazy ride that has now taken Marsh and Levi to three countries. It's been a joy to see you embrace and love these two as much as I do. It makes writing them all the more rewarding.

Finishing and publishing this book, however, was not easy. I could not have done it without my husband. Day job deadlines, COVID, a home purchase, and a cross-country move all conspired to try to delay this book. When I thought I would have to do just that, my husband said, "Just get it done." And so I did, with his help and with the help of my incredible team:

Cate Ashwood, Wander Aguiar, and Steven Dehler for the sexy cover.

Susie Selva on edits, Lori Parks on proofreading, Kim on beta notes.

Nina, the VPR Team, Leslie, and the GRR Team on publicity.

Christian Leatherman for lending his voice and giving Marsh, Levi, and all my characters a whole new layer of depth and excitement.

And all the sprint partners and cheerleaders who kept me going, especially Annabeth, Allison, Erin, Aimee, Toshi, Kim, Rachel, and the Lushes.

Much love and thanks to you all!

ALSO BY LAYLA REYNE

For the most up-to-date list of titles and a helpful reading order, please visit www.laylareyne.com.

Perfect Play:

Dead Draw

Bad Bishop

King Hunt

Fog City:

Prince of Killers

King Slayer

A New Empire

Queen's Ransom

Silent Knight

Agents Irish and Whiskey:

Single Malt

Cask Strength

Barrel Proof

Tequila Sunrise

Trouble Brewing:

Imperial Stout

Craft Brew

Noble Hops

Standalone Titles:

Variable Onset

What We May Be

Changing Lanes:

Relay

Medley

Table for Two:

The Last Drop

Dine With Me

Free Stories:

Freestyle

Blended Whiskey

Final Gravity

Sweater Weather

ABOUT THE AUTHOR

Layla Reyne is the author of *What We May Be* and the *Perfect Play*, *Fog City*, and *Agents Irish and Whiskey* series. A Carolina Tar Heel who spent fifteen years in California, Layla enjoys weaving her bicoastal experiences into her stories, along with adrenaline-fueled suspense and heart pounding romance.

You can find Layla at laylareyne.com, in her reader group on Facebook—Layla's Lushes, and at the following sites:

facebook.com/laylareyne

twitter.com/laylareyne

instagram.com/laylareyne

bookbub.com/authors/layla-reyne

www.ingramcontent.com/pod-product-compliance
Lightning Source LLC
Chambersburg PA
CBHW071431200726
48294CB00002B/588